Trust Me,

I'm a Banker

TRUST ME, I'M A BANKER

◆ ◆

David Charters

◆

Photographs by
Alice Rosenbaum

Elliott & Thompson
London

For Ella, my bambolina

Author's Note and Acknowledgements

Just when it seemed safe to return to the Square Mile, Dave Hart is back. Having very nearly finished him off at the end of *Bonus Time*, I was surprised that a lot of people wanted to see him again.

Readers should know that this *is* a work of fiction. Dave is my City anti-hero, the man who embodies all that was worst in all of the worst people I came across in my investment banking career. The bank he joins, Erste Frankfurter Grossbank, is a fictional combination of many of the sleepier European banks from the early nineties, with all of their faults and virtues, rather than representing any one particular firm.

Alice Rosenbaum has again woven her sinister magic around the world of the investment banker, this time turning her lens on Frankfurt as well as London. She has an uncanny knack for uncovering the dark side of what seems a familiar world.

A number of people provided generous advice and help during the writing of *Trust Me, I'm a Banker*: Lorne Forsyth, Andreas Haindl, Joerg Illhardt, Roger Lewis, Jane Miller, Joanna Rice, Adam Shutkever, my sister Margaret and my oldest son Mark all deserve special mention, and of course Luisa, my wife, who supported me throughout the process and did her best to keep me sane.

What would it take to make you kill someone?

I'm standing in the glass-box corner office of Rory, my fair-haired, blue-eyed boy wonder of a boss, waiting for him to gratify himself at my expense, waiting for him to enjoy his moment of supreme power and domination of another human being. That human being is me. It's bonus time, and he's about to pay me.

Only this year it's different.

This year I've had enough. This year the pressure is too much. The waiting has nearly killed me. All my hopes, all my aspirations, have gone out of the window. He was going to nail me, and laugh at my expense.

It doesn't help that Wendy, my beautiful, high-spending, attractive, money-loving, high maintenance wife, has left me for her personal trainer, probably figuring that she's spent the bonus year with me, as well as all the other years, and she'll collect handsomely for 'our' achievements. Or maybe she's figured that it isn't worth hanging around. It doesn't help either that she's taken Samantha with her, our darling three year old, the apple of her father's eye, the child for whom I could never buy enough.

So I'm alone. A man who has lost everything. A man who has become dangerous. And in my briefcase, with the lid open so that Rory can't see it, is a machete. A special machete, bought in the Africa Sale at Christie's, used by explorers carving out the Dark Continent. It's going to carve something else now. I'm about to slice Rory's neatly coiffed skull wide open. That's why I closed the blinds when I came in, shutting off the view to the trading floor. It's payback time.

Rory has left the list of departmental bonuses on the desk in front of him, so that I can see it. He wants me to know that at twenty-five thousand pounds, I'm setting a new record for a managing director at the firm. I'm to be paid the lowest bonus of all time.

So I do what investment bankers always do in meetings. Even though I don't mean it, I smile. And as I swivel the briefcase round so that he can see what's inside, I lean forward across the desk, grasping the handle of the machete.

It's a perfect moment. Rory's eyes follow mine to the briefcase, widen as they take in the machete, his mouth drops open, and he turns and stares back at me.

I nod and grin. Over the years I've done a lot of nodding and grinning at Rory, smiling as he told me I had to do another all-nighter, or cancel a holiday, or that the bonus couldn't be quite what I was expecting because Fixed Income had had a tough year, or there were big losses in private equity, or whatever. But this time I'm grinning because I'm in charge. In the world of executive aggression, I'm breaking the rules. I'm introducing the real thing. And the man with the machete is always boss.

The colour has drained beautifully from Rory's normally tanned face, and his Adam's apple is bobbing up and down in his throat. He's facing a madman. Harvard Business School doesn't teach you what to do next, does it, Rory?

'Dave… wait…' He raises a placating hand, and at the same time pushes his chair back from the desk. His eyes flicker across to the door, but the beauty of one of these large corner offices is that the door is a long way from the desk. A long way to savour the discomfort of the wretched people summoned here sweating to be told the result of a whole year of their lives. A long way to cover, with a madman swinging a machete at you.

All I do is grin. I never knew this could be so much fun. He's human, just like the rest of us. And he's shitting himself. Quite why he ever thought he could carry on messing with real people's lives the way he did is beyond me. Out there on the street, people get mugged for a walletful of notes. In here we're talking millions. What would you do for millions?

'Dave – we need to talk about this.' His mouth is dry. He's finding it hard to get the words out, and joy of joys, he's perspiring.

I shake my head. 'Talking's over.'

'Dave – I have a wife, children – please don't do anything rash.'

'This isn't rash. I've had a long time to think about this.'

'Dave – we're investment bankers. Investment bankers don't kill each other.'

'The rules just changed.' My voice is a whisper, but it's totally calm, not a hint of the excitement, the bloodlust, the adrenaline pumping through me. Rory crumples at his desk and puts his head in his hands. His shoulders start heaving to and fro and a strange noise comes from him. I look at him, vaguely embarrassed. He's sobbing.

And then the door opens.

The bubble bursts as a film crew appears. There are three of them. They are led by a tall, skinny woman with mousy hair wearing a dark grey trouser suit who looks almost but not quite beautiful in an uptight, bossy, reporter-like way. She is flanked by a scruffy, shaggy haired camera man and an even taller, skinny guy in jeans and a T-shirt, carrying what looks like a very large sound recorder and a long-handled microphone. Behind them, Rory's PA is trying to get past, looking apologetic. Before she can get a word in, the woman, whom I've recognised as a pushy dimwit who asks idiotic questions on NTV Cable Business News, marches across the room with her hand thrust out.

'Amie Short – we're here to do the piece on this year's bonus round in the City. Which of you is Rory?'

Possibly for the first time in my life, I experience one of those moments when everything happens very slowly. Rory has leapt to his feet, knocking over his chair, and I watch as he rushes forward to grasp her hand in both of his, swivelling her around so that she's standing between him and me. She doesn't know it, but she's his human shield.

'Me – I'm Rory, that's me. Welcome, come in, all of you, come in.'

His voice is unnaturally squeaky and high-pitched, he's breathing hard, and he has sweat patches under his arms.

For a deliciously crazy moment I wonder whether to bring the machete out of my briefcase and start swinging and slashing at everyone in the room. I imagine blood splashing over the carpet and the blinds and the desk, limbs and lumps of raw meat flying around so the place looks like an abattoir. I imagine standing triumphantly amidst the corpses – 'NTV Cable Business News regrets to announce the death of our reporter Amie Short and her film crew. Amie was covering this year's bonus round at Bartons, the blue chip UK investment bank, when she got caught in the middle of a discussion between star investment banker Dave Hart and his boss…' But instead, I drop the machete back into the briefcase and click it shut, closing the lid that shielded it from the film crew.

Rory is standing, panting, next to Amie, ignoring her, staring at me. She's looking at him curiously, and follows his glance in my direction.

'Are we interrupting something?'

No, of course not, you brain-dead moron. Try rubbing both brain cells together and see if you get a spark. I was just about to kill my boss, you dimwit. It's the sort of thing that happens at this time of year. Or at least this year.

I smile confidently and nod back. 'No, no problem.' I turn to Rory. 'I think we'd covered the ground. Rory, I'll see you another time. We need to pick up where we left off. Maybe I'll pop around to your place tonight? Or if not tonight, then some other time. I'm sure I'll catch you again.'

He just stares at me, open-mouthed, to the obvious puzzlement of the film crew. I walk purposefully out of his office, swing by my desk to grab my jacket from the back of the chair, smiling at the team, who have probably been laying bets on how I would do, and head out of the building fast, before Rory can wake up and call security.

It's only when I emerge from the Underground in Sloane Square and dump the machete in a rubbish bin, having wiped the handle fastidiously with my handkerchief and wrapped it in a newspaper, that I realise I've utterly blown it.

If you're going to kill your boss, you really have to do it. No half measures. I return to my empty, barren flat and start re-running the whole scene in my mind over and over again. I knew what I had to do, but I couldn't even get that right.

Without Wendy and Samantha, the flat seems soulless. Half the cupboards and wardrobes are empty. All the familiar sounds and smells are gone. I spend the rest of the day moping around the place, wallowing in depression, waiting for the doorbell to ring and armed police to arrest the maniac who thought he could kill his boss. I stare at myself in the mirror, noting the first grey hairs at thirty-seven years of age, the lines on my face, the slightly sagging belly. How did it all happen?

But then I start to wonder. I'm an investment banker, after all, and we're nothing if not resilient. The doorbell hasn't rung, neither has the phone, and when I fire up the computer and log in to my e-mails, it's all routine stuff, some banter from the team about the bonus round, but nothing about me. Then I start to think about the situation. What will Rory do? What can he do? Make some crazy allegations? Where's the proof? Who would believe him? Of all the people in the world, Dave Hart must be the least likely ever to bite back. And if they didn't believe him, and I was still out here, on the loose, watching and waiting and knowing where he lives – I have the addresses of all of his homes – he'd be the one who was scared. In the safely cocooned, insulated world of the global investment banker, no-one actually gets hurt – at least not physically.

Finally at around five o'clock I make a decision. I experience a burst of what is known in the markets as irrational exuberance. I was going to kill my boss, but I didn't. And so far, I've got away with it. Nothing's happened. I'm a free man, and who knows what possibilities lie ahead? I go out and buy a half case of champagne, plus whisky, vodka and gin, replenishing the stocks that I've exhausted over the previous weeks of uncertainty, call up a couple of drinking buddies and decide to have a party. It may be the last party I'll ever have, so I might as well make it good – the condemned man and all that.

The buddies I call up are Dan Harriman, who runs European equities at Hardman Stoney, and Nigel Farmer, the number two on the oil trading desk at Berkmann Schliebowitz. Both are single men, in the sense that they are divorced –

Dan recently for the second time – and both know how to party. You might think three guys sitting around in my flat drinking is a pretty sad sort of party, but I haven't told you about the hookers.

Hookers? Well, no, not exactly. Escorts. High-class escorts. These days you can find them on the internet, whole galleries full of them. Not the firm's internet of course – the firewall stops you browsing from the office. That's why we all have these rinky-dink, tiny personal laptops with Wi-Fi connections. You didn't think all those young men sitting on public benches in the 'Wi-Fi village' at Canary Wharf were checking stock prices, did you?

And let's be absolutely clear what happens when you book these girls. You're paying for their time and company only. Anything else that happens is a private matter between consenting adults. Yes, really.

So around ten o'clock that night, Dan is sitting on the sofa in my living room, his shirt off, exposing his flabby, hairy belly, his trousers and underpants around his ankles, and blonde-haired, twenty-three year old Ilyana from Kiev is going down on him. Nigel, similarly half-dressed, is standing by the drinks cabinet, pouring himself another large Scotch, while dark-haired Carla, twenty-one, from Brazil kneels at his feet and services him. I'm totally naked, sitting in the large armchair, while red-haired Helena from Warsaw straddles me. On the rug in front of the fireplace Patricia from Spain, a brunette whose hair reaches almost to her waist, and Beatrice, a beautiful black girl from Columbia, are lying head to toe, servicing each other for our entertainment and pleasure. All of the girls are naked, obviously, and their clothes and lingerie are scattered around the apartment, on the furniture, on the floor, a g-string here, a micro-bra there. Half empty champagne bottles and glasses are similarly spread around, there's a suspicious scattering of white powder on the glass coffee table, and on the huge, flat screen wall-mounted TV over the fireplace there's a hard-core movie showing a stunning blonde from California kneeling on all fours and being serviced at both ends by a couple of studs who are hung like gorillas.

You might think this is the kind of thing that goes on every night in those exclusive apartments around Sloane Square, but in fact I haven't partied like this since before I was married. Honestly. At least not at home.

The drugs and the porn were not my idea. Dan brought those. I don't use drugs, and I regard porn as a poor substitute for the real thing. The escorts, okay, I take some of the blame, but how was I to know what these girls would do? And the only reason investment bankers get dragged into these murky areas is because their clients want it. Honestly.

So there we were, the party in full swing, and it wasn't yet late, when I could swear I heard a key in the front door. I look past Helena, who is moaning and groaning at the top of her voice, throwing her head around, rolling her eyes and doing an amazing fake orgasm impression, and there, standing shocked and amazed in the entrance to the living room, is Wendy. She's wearing a sober dark grey skirt and jacket by Armani, with a white silk blouse, and discreet emerald and pearl earrings from Elizabeth Gage. She looks stylish and beautiful in an understated, luxurious way. And terribly small, frightened and vulnerable. My heart goes out to her and for a sickening moment I think I can remember why I fell in love with her.

'What… is going on?' Christ. She's shaking her head as she takes in the scene around her, and giving me one of those 'this is too horrible, I just can't believe it' looks.

Dan looks up from the sofa, and reaches across for his crumpled jacket, momentarily ignoring the bobbing head in his lap. He's got a crazy look on his sweaty, florid face. He pulls out his wallet and looks up at Wendy.

'Here's five hundred quid. Get your kit off. Bend over the coffee table and I'll have you next.' Dan's never met Wendy. He's holding out a pile of notes, and frowns as she screams and fixes me with a half-crazed stare.

'I wanted to come back! I wanted to stand by you! I wanted to give you a second chance!' She turns and runs back towards the front door.

'Wendy! Darling! This isn't what you think…'
The front door slams and Dan looks at me and shrugs. 'Women…'

♦ ♦ ♦

I need to get away. Anywhere. Fast.

I've hardly slept since Dan and Nigel and the last of the girls left, around three a.m. Yes, that's right – three a.m. Of course we carried on partying after Wendy left. What else could we do? We'd all taken Viagra – my one concession to chemical assistance - there were five girls already in the apartment, with a new shift due to arrive at midnight, and we were flying.

But now it's eight a.m., I've hardly slept and there are ugly monsters crawling out of the darkest corners of my mind, monsters with names like conscience and trust and integrity. I think if I stay here any longer I'll go mad.

And what if the police come? Rory's had a whole night to ponder what to do. I bet he hasn't slept either. Should I call him? By now he'll probably have his phone lines monitored. He's not a man to under-estimate. What if he's hired someone to come after me?

That makes me think. Could he? In the movies he would. But in real life, if you don't mix with the criminal classes – other than smart, white collar crimi-nals, who don't actually hurt people, but do things like running hedge funds and dealing on insider information – how would you know where to go to hire a hit-man? That's one service you can't yet order over the internet.

I'm spooked. I admit it. I rush frenetically around the flat, picking up used condoms, clearing away empty bottles and glasses, hoover up every last trace of powder around the coffee table, search under the cushions for Ilyana's missing g-string and put it down the waste disposal, and finally collapse, exhausted and still feeling guilty, and stare around my prison cell. The terrifying thought strikes me that it could so easily be swapped for a real prison cell, and investment bankers just don't do prison. Prison is for little people, the great unwashed, the huge unwealthy masses who toil in the industries whose fate we decide with our clever deal-making skills. It's not for us, at least as long as we stick to the unspoken code. But I didn't. Machetes aren't covered by the code.

I need to leave town. Somewhere hot, far away, with a beach, a complete change of scene, and of course hot and cold running nymphettes. I know where I need to go. Hardman Stoney had their MDs' off-site there last year, and Dan can give me the low-down on the local scene. I go on-line, make a few calls, and to my surprise and good fortune strike lucky, picking up a last minute cancellation. I pack a bag and call a cab to take me to Heathrow. I figure that I've lost my job – I can't see Rory having me back – and with my debts and overdraft, the balance of the mortgage, and my imminent divorce, I'm as close to being insolvent as anyone who plays in the high stakes casino of the Square Mile and loses. So I do the obvious thing, use my corporate credit card – amazingly still working, what is Rory (not) doing?! – and book a First Class ticket. Jamaica beckons – Caribbean sunshine, reggae music and nubile black bodies. I have to escape.

It's the pre-Christmas rush, and when I get to Heathrow, thousands of wannabe holidaymakers are thronging in the departure hall. My Gold Card doesn't help, because I haven't had time to pick up a ticket, and need to queue to get an e-ticket from a machine. When I finally do get my ticket, I need to queue again to get some currency – Jamaican dollars for out of pockets, and US dollars, as the global currency of available young women everywhere. Then, privilege of privileges, I get to queue again, this time for security. After all this, I get to line up to board. I'm late, and there doesn't seem to be a separate line for First Class passengers to go ahead of the waiting throng.

In front of me in the line is the family from hell. The father, who I gather by eavesdropping is called Mick, is a forty-something, shaven-headed thug in a tracksuit and perfectly unblemished white trainers – presumably freshly shoplifted for the holiday from Lilywhites or bought from 'some bloke down the pub, can't remember his name, officer, honestly' - with an earring and a sour, hostile look on his face. The mother is a flabby beast soaked in an overwhelming aura of cheap scent and wearing tight pink leggings and a bulging white vest that leaves her bare arms and shoulders exposed to show off her tattoos. I can tell she's an ugly slapper with attitude just by looking at her – I don't need her to tattoo herself to spell it out. Jason and Kennie are aged about seven and nine, just old enough to have acquired their father's surly resentment. *You lookin' at me? You want some?* Despite their age, every second word starts with an 'f', until their mother catches my eye and tells them to 'stop that bloody swearing'. I'm wearing a blazer from Brooks Brothers, slacks and an open shirt from Gieves and Hawkes, with tan leather lace-up shoes from Fratelli Rossetti. To her I probably look like some kind of authority figure. She looks back to me, as if for approval, but I turn away, scowling.

What pisses me off most, apart from the fact that I have to stand next to them, is that they probably all live on benefits, paid for out of taxes raised from people like me. In fact, when I think about all the money I've paid in taxes in recent years, even without getting anything like my fair due at bonus time, I probably support a whole village full of idiots. And Rory, well he must support a couple of large towns of these people. Maybe they should name one after him, or call all of their first-born sons Rory? Between the MD's at the firm, we must support a whole county. Add in the other top investment banks, and the hedge fund industry, and the pension funds and insurance companies in the City, and pretty soon you're funding a whole underclass of work-shy, uneducated, irretrievably incapable parasites. All they can do is consume and breed and occasionally fight, while someone else picks up the tab. People in the real world may not like the privileged élite who work in the Square Mile, but what would they do without us? Who else would pay for their social failures, allowing them to indulge in the notion of a caring society? Let's hear it for capitalism.

Behind me is another family, and they're almost as bad. Toby, Jasper and Monty must be aged between four and eight, wholesome, well-scrubbed, terribly well-spoken well beyond their years, and immaculately dressed in identical clothing from some middle-class mail order catalogue. Their pretty, tired but enthusiastic, cheerful in adversity, long-haired thirty-something mother is wearing loose, practical trousers and a white blouse and cardigan, probably from Marks and Spencer, and is actually holding hands with her very tall, slightly other worldly, professorial husband, who's staring around the departure hall, as if he hasn't been in one before. They are the hard-working, fair-minded, serious, law-abiding, aspiring lower middle classes at their nauseatingly cheerful worst. Announce that there's a six hour flight delay, and they'll shrug their shoulders and say, 'Oh well, never mind. Let's see where we can sit down – isn't this exciting, children?' and start to play 'I spy' while mum gets out packs of home-made sandwiches and a flask of tea. They are probably schoolteachers, or civil servants at the Department of Social Security. For all I know he might even be a vicar, and no matter how well they do, how hard they work, they'll never know what it feels like to make a million dollars at bonus time. In their world, it simply doesn't happen.

I'm too young to be a grumpy old man, and I know it's wrong to sneer – though I've never quite worked out why – but people like this make me sick. They lead plodding, one-track lives, where the most exceptional thing that happens is falling in love, getting married, having kids, raising them, and launching a whole new, self-perpetuating cycle. Eventually they have grandchildren and then they die, without ever making a bean. What are these people for?

I'm beginning to feel stressed by the delay, so much so that I start taking deep, relaxing breaths. What if I can't actually leave the country? What if the inscrutable official at the desk looks at my passport, glances briefly at me and presses some hidden button to call the police to take me away? 'Fugitive investment banker caught at Heathrow' – I can see the headlines now.

There's a commotion ahead. A lot of people are shouting, and some are moving forward, crowding around what looks like a middle-aged man lying on the ground. Women are saying things like 'Oh, my God', and one of the airline ground staff is making an urgent phone call from the check-in desk.

I can't bear this any longer.

'Excuse me! May I come through?' I surprise myself with the strength of my voice, as I step forward and the crowd parts and people look at me expectantly. 'Excuse me – may I come past? Thank you.' They automatically step aside as they hear a voice of authority. Several people are kneeling helplessly beside a grey-haired man in a crumpled tropical suit. He looks very pale and it's not clear if he's still breathing.

'Are you a doctor?'

'No.' I step forward, lifting my feet carefully over the prone victim of what I suppose must be a heart attack, and present myself at check-in. 'I'm an investment banker.' I turn to the check-in attendant. 'Dave Hart, seat 1A.'

There's a buzz of angry conversation behind me, and the check-in girl seems reluctant at first to take my passport and ticket, but I stare her out and she finally lets me through. I can feel a wave of hatred hitting my back from the crowd as I walk down the jetty towards the waiting airliner. Some people would be bothered by this, but not me. I have investment banker's immunity to the feelings of the Little People. This is a result. Instead of standing in line like some gormless twerp, I can get on board, relax and order my first glass of champagne.

♦ ♦ ♦

I'm on my third glass, munching canapés, sitting in the best seat on the plane – seat 1A, the only one that Rory would consider on the rare occasions when he used public transport, rather than taking the corporate jet. I've booked a suite at the Bay Club, Jamaica's hottest new property, with scuba diving, water skiing, tennis, golf, a Givenchy spa, and the closest thing you'll find to *haute cuisine* dining in the English-speaking Caribbean. I've also got Dan Harriman's list of hot numbers to call. I may be a fugitive from justice, as well as from my soon-to-be-ex-wife, with no job, no prospects, and no future, but life is good, at least for the moment. First Class is almost empty, which is how I like it. Just a few business types quietly sipping champagne and reading.

The plane was thirty minutes late taking off, because they had to remove the bags of a passenger who had been taken seriously ill before take-off. I'm philosophical about these things. It allows me time to chat to a very pretty blonde stewardess called Maxine, who's half-French, has small boobs and a cute backside. It's all going really well, until she explains that the announcement they've just made isn't strictly accurate. The man who was taken ill actually died. And one of the First Class passengers apparently stepped over him in order not to be delayed at check-in, while he was actually dying! We look around at the other passengers and wonder who it might be. After that I lose interest in Maxine.

I glance at the curtain that separates First Class from the rest of the plane. Back there in World Cattlemarket Class I can imagine Mick and Jason and Kennie arguing over who gets the last plastic chicken korma from the trolley, while Toby, Jason and Monty munch contentedly on mum's sandwiches, probably made with gluten-free, organic wholemeal bread, low-fat margarine and cold breast of free-range chicken. Any time now the adults will be served their last alcoholic drinks, the lights will be dimmed, the air conditioning turned off so that the cabin gets hot and stuffy, and the cattle will doze off and start snoring for the duration. Gross.

There is a story that Rory once took his family on a holiday to Australia. Naturally, they all had seats in First Class, along with the nanny and the au pair. But it was a long flight and the kids started misbehaving. Rory, as a man accustomed to being in charge of his destiny, found this all a bit too much and finally lost it, threatening the kids that if they didn't behave, he'd send them 'back there' – he pointed to the curtain – where they'd never been before. His kids were pretty scared and took a peep behind the curtains. All they'd ever done in their lives was board an aircraft and turn left. They didn't know what happened if you turned right, and probably thought that behind the curtains on the right was where the baggage was kept, and the fuel was stored, and where the engines were. When they saw there were actually whole rows of people asleep back there, they really freaked out, got the point and came back to sit down and be quiet for the rest of the flight. It made a real impact on them. They were terrified.

And the best thing of all? They weren't even looking at Economy Class. Behind the curtain was Business Class, where Rory made the rest of us sit on corporate trips.

After dinner and a movie, I doze for a while and finally wake up to the welcome news that we'll be landing in half an hour. As a jaded long-haul traveller, I don't usually get excited any more about flying, but this trip is different. I feel like a kid who's been let out of school early.

In the baggage hall I grab a porter, and I'm delighted to see that First Class baggage really does come off before Mick's. I watch while Jason and Kennie climb all over the carousel, and wonder if it will start up and slice their fingers off. They look sweaty and filthy, their T-shirts covered in the spilt remains of whatever food they were served in-flight. Toby, Jasper and Monty are still looking well scrubbed – probably cleaned off by mum in the toilets half an hour before landing, while dad – the vicar – is staring around the arrivals lounge, obviously never having seen one before.

I'm through Immigration in a flash – no arrest warrants here – and a beaming black man in a white suit is holding a name card with 'Mr D Hart – Bay Club' on it. While Mick is still waiting for his baggage, I'm in the back of an air-conditioned stretch limo, sipping a glass of mineral water so cold that I fear it could crack the enamel on my teeth. This is living.

♦ ♦ ♦

I hate the Bay Club.

For starters, they don't allow hookers. Why any businessman would ever stay here is beyond me. On my second night, after conquering my jet-lag, and with no sign that anyone was after me from the UK, I decided to have a party. Not quite on the scale of my last party in London, but a party nevertheless. I made a couple of phone calls, took a shower, put on my hotel dressing gown, and sat on the sofa in my suite nursing a large Scotch and water. Then the phone rang.

'Mister Hart?'

'Who is it?'

'It's reception, sir. There are two…'

There was an awkward pause. 'Yes?'

'There are two… young ladies here. They are asking for you, Mister Hart.'

'Excellent. They must be my nieces.' I chuckle knowingly, as if sharing an in-joke with the man on reception. 'Why don't you show them up?' I've used this line before, and generally it works. The guy on reception knows they aren't my nieces, and he knows that I know that he knows. And what I'm suggesting is that he shows them up, rather than sending them up, because obviously I'm going to slip him a couple of large denomination notes for being accommodating.

'I'm sorry, Mister Hart, but it's against hotel policy.'

'What? Are you saying hotel guests can't entertain visitors in their suites?' I raise my voice to emphasise the point. 'In their thousand-dollar-a-night suites?'

'I'm afraid so, Mister Hart. Would you like to speak to the night manager?'

'Certainly not. I want to speak to you. Right now. In person. Kindly come up straight away, and bring the young ladies with you.' As I say this, I reach over to my wallet and reluctantly start unpeeling hundred dollar bills. Whoever this fellow is, he takes his job seriously. This is going to be expensive.

'That's not possible, Mister Hart. I'm sending the young ladies away. There are many other attractions at the Bay Club, Mister Hart. Have you tried the Givenchy facial, or the pedicure? Or how about a golf lesson? Or tennis?'

I can't believe I'm hearing this. 'Do you know who I am?' I positively roar the words down the phone. There's a pause at the other end, and then a different, older voice comes on the line.

'We know exactly who you are, Mister Hart.' This totally freaks me out. Who is this? What does he know? How can he know anything at all about me? I only got here two days ago. 'And you must know that an upmarket family resort hotel cannot allow ladies of this type on the premises.'

I hang up. Damn, I swallowed a Viagra tablet forty minutes ago. Swallow them quickly, they say, in case you get a stiff neck. I should have waited until the girls showed up. Now I daren't even go down to the bar for a drink in case I embarrass myself. And what about the girls? Who will pay for their taxi out to the resort, or pay them for their time, or their trip home? I imagine some vengeful Yardie pimp with a revolver slipping into my room at night and firing round after round into my sleeping body. I sit in my room, torturing myself and steadily draining the mini-bar.

The next day at breakfast I have the feeling that everyone is looking at me. Not just the staff, but somehow I get the sense that the guests know all about the scene last night at reception, when a couple of hookers were turned away. A couple of hookers? Yes, that's right. He wanted two of them, the twisted, perverted beast. I look across at the elderly couple spooning up mouthfuls of muesli at the table on my right. They nod cheerfully and smile 'Good morning', but I know that they know.

After breakfast I wander over to the pool to lie in the sun and snooze. Amazingly, every sun-lounger is taken. I look around and can see nothing but an oil slick of nearly naked Germans, Scandinavians and Dutch people, roasting slowly in the Caribbean sun. Where do they come from so early in the day, and how do they get all the best places?

I wander down to the beach, which is the private property of the hotel, but runs alongside a public beach that is open to anyone. Sure enough, members of the public are wandering across our beach. And then it gets worse. Mick is here, with Kennie and Jason, and his appallingly bovine wife.

'Hey, Mister – wasn't you on the same plane as us? Wasn't you the one what stepped over that bloke what was dying?' Kennie is looking up at me from the deep, possibly deadly pit the male members of the family are excavating. It's already up to his chest, and must have taken real labour. Perhaps Mick isn't just a benefits parasite, but works as well, as some of the more enterprising ones do, and digs up roads or operates a digger machine in his working life?

I ignore Kennie and stare out to sea, imagining that I must cut a romantic figure, dressed in my Villebrequin shorts, my Ralph Lauren polo shirt and my Rayban shades – echoes of Tom Cruise.

'We're staying at the Coconut Club – the other side of the bay from this place.' It's a gruff male voice, estuary English, and I realise that Mick is talking to me. 'The beach isn't as nice there, so we come here instead. Belongs to this posh place, but they can't stop us, see?'

Feeling trapped, I reluctantly acknowledge him. 'Really?'

'You bet. And there's a barbecue here tomorrow night as well.' He winks conspiratorially. 'Might even see if we can slip in.'

'Good idea.'

'By the way, that fella died.'

'Really?'

'Stone cold dead. "Brown bread," as we say down our way. In case you was interested.'

'Not really.' I find this exchange slightly surreal. Is he trying to prick my conscience in his slovenly, uncouth way? Doubtful. Probably just trying to make conversation. Under other circumstances, the first thing I'd do would be to tip-off hotel security about gatecrashers at the following night's beach barbecue, but

I'm so fed up with the hotel, with the nearly naked Germans, Dutch and Scandinavians, and with the prospect of spending a thousand dollars a night in order not to get laid, that I actually chuckle.

'See you at the barbecue.'

Mick grins and gives me the thumbs up.

I wander along the beach, and it gets worse. The Wholesome Family are here too. Toby, Jasper and Monty splashing in the waves while the vicar stares at people making sandcastles as if he hasn't seen them before, and Missus Wholesome spreads out a blanket and starts slicing up a melon and putting pieces onto brightly coloured paper plates that she must have bought in a local supermarket.

'Weren't we on the same plane?' She looks up and smiles as I walk past.

I shake my head. 'No. You must have seen my cousin, Dan Harriman. Flew out a couple of days ago. We look very similar. He's a total shit, steps over dying people if they're in his way, does drugs, hookers, booze, you name it. Even tried to smash his boss's head in with a machete.'

She tilts her head on one side to stare at me, and I realise that under other circumstances she might be quite attractive – well, at least shaggable – and she laughs. 'It was you. You stepped over…'

'Don't tell me. I stepped over a dying man. I know I stepped over a dying man, although I didn't know then that he was dying, and realistically there was nothing I could do even if I did know. I'm not a doctor, and I'm not a first-aider. At least by getting out of his way I could give him some privacy. And dignity. It's better than standing round gawping at him.'

'Don't sound so defensive. You weren't to know.' She has long brown hair tied up in a bun, freckles and a delightful snub nose. She's definitely fuckable.

'I'm not. Just rational. Are you staying at the Coconut Club with…' I nod towards Mick and his family.

'With Mick? Yes. He told us about this beach. Apparently there's a barbecue tomorrow night, and he wants us all to gatecrash it. But I don't think Trevor wants to.'

Trevor? I might have known her husband would be called Trevor. He looks like a Trevor.

'Well, I'm actually staying here. I have a suite. Tell Trevor you can all be my guests. See you around eight?'

'We'd love to. Are you sure it's all right if we all come?' She stands up and holds out her hand. 'I'm Sally by the way. Sally Mills.'

I shake her hand and find she has a delightfully firm grip. I love it when women have a firm grip. Anyway, she's wearing a conservative one-piece swimsuit that covers up rather too much and has never been seen by any designer known to man, yet still she looks attractive. For a moment I imagine lying on my back on my bed in the hotel, while a naked Sally Mills sits on my face and goes down on me.

'Pleased to meet you. See you tomorrow. Let's hope it's a big night.'

'Let's.' She smiles and catches my eye, and I wonder briefly if she's flirting. Well, what woman wouldn't, if she met me, on a beach in the Caribbean? Tom Cruise's half-brother. Especially if she was married to Trevor the teacher.

◆ ◆ ◆

I'm flying.

We've got a big table near the barbecue, just a few yards from an improvised dance floor that's been put together on the beach, and waiters are running a shuttle service of cocktails from the bar. Mick has helpfully sat himself next to Trevor, and keeps making him drink more, which he's obviously not used to, while Mick's wife, Claire the Human Pudding, is on Trevor's other side, keeping him wedged in. The kids are all over the place, running round causing havoc.

I'm playing the role of perfect host. I greeted everyone when they arrived, and made them all laugh by explaining how there'd been a bit of tension at the hotel. Apparently the Germans and the Dutch and the Scandinavians were in the habit of going out to the pool last thing at night, and spreading out their towels and magazines and personal odds and ends on the loungers to claim the best sunbathing spots. Well, last night someone went out even later and threw all the Dutch and Scandinavians' things in the pool, leaving only the Germans'. Outrageous, what some people will do, and this morning it nearly caused world war three. We all have a laugh, Mick gives me a sideways glance, but I don't react, and instead we settle down to drinking, which I'm quite good at.

A steel band is playing, and the beach is beautifully lit with burning torches, under a clear, starlit sky. I'm feeling so good about life that I even gaze on benevolently when some of the Germans and the Scandinavians start to heal the tension with a little friendly limbo dancing.

The reason I'm so particularly happy is sitting opposite me, her view of Trevor blocked by the bulk of the Human Pudding, and we're talking as if no-one else is around.

'Investment banking is a tough business.'

'Really?'

'Sure. The hours are a killer, when we're on a deal we work till we drop. I once did three all-nighters in a row. You work weekends, you start by seven in the morning, and if you're lucky you finish by midnight. You travel all over the world, everywhere the business is. It's brutally competitive, everyone's bright, everyone's hard-working, everyone wants to win. Imagine a whole trading floor of alpha males – and females, we have women investment bankers too – and every one of them is convinced he can run the firm. Testosterone on steroids.'

'Sounds exciting.'

'You bet.' I pause to drain my marguerita, then raise the glass and signal to a waiter for another. 'You never know what's going to happen from one moment to the next. It's the market, you see. The market's bigger than any of us. War, terrorism, politics, everything's reflected in the market. You need perfect news flow, and seconds, not minutes, make all the difference. Blink and you're left behind.' I smile in acknowledgement as another glass is placed in front of me. 'But it takes its toll.'

'Oh?'

I put on my sad, mournful look. 'Things didn't work out at home. I'm getting divorced. That's why I'm here… alone.'

'Really? Because of your work?'

No, you silly cow, because I'm a shallow, greedy, philandering piss-head without a decent bone in his body. 'I'm afraid so. And the worst of it is, I won't be able to see my beautiful Samantha again.'

'Samantha?'

'My daughter. She's three.' I could add that she's the one I haven't even thought about until now, when I realised what a great sympathy card she is, and sympathy could be a great way into those no doubt brilliant white, practical cotton panties.

'Won't you be able to see her?'

I shrug and stare into the darkness. 'You know what it's like. It's not exactly an even-handed system.' And thank God for that – what would I do with Samantha for a whole weekend without Wendy around?

'I'm sorry.' Her voice is a whisper, and it looks as if she has tears in her eyes. She glances around to check on her own boys, as if to reassure herself that Toby, Jasper and Monty are not in danger of being whisked away.

'Don't be. I've learnt to be tough. You have to be in my business. I'll get through it. It's just that sometimes you have to let your guard down, you have to open up to someone. It's pretty rare that you find someone you can trust, or feel close to.' As I say this, I look into her eyes. Even in the light of the blazing torches I can see her blush as she glances away. Time for a change of mood.

'Anyway, that's enough about me. Let's talk about you.'

I smile reassuringly. 'What do you think about me?'

That's when somebody screams.

For once it isn't something I've said. We turn and see a group of tall, rangy men with dreadlocks standing on the makeshift dance floor built out over the sand. The band have stopped playing and in the silence we can hear someone moaning. There's a body lying on the dance floor, and I think I recognise it as one of the hotel security men. There are six or seven men standing over him, and they are all carrying weapons – knives, baseball bats, and one of them has a machete.

Suddenly Sally screams, as the man with the machete leans forward and sweeps up a small bundle from the floor beside him. Toby, aged four years and three months, screams 'Mummy!' as the man shouts at us in a spaced-out, half-crazed, vaguely sing-song Jamaican accent, 'Ladies and gentlemen – please be so kind as to hand over your wallets and your watches and your jewellery to my associates. Please be so kind and we all be cool…'

A surprisingly strong hand grasps the sleeve of my collarless white Armani evening shirt and yanks me out of my chair.

'He's got Toby – come on!' Sally Mills might only weigh a little over fifty kilos, but she has the strength of a man possessed. She pulls me out of my chair and drags me forward alongside her as she charges towards the dance floor.

Only she trips up on the sand and falls headlong, releasing her grasp of my shirt in time to catapult me into the dreadlocked gangster holding Toby. I'm wearing a brand new pair of navy blue Gucci loafers and shouldn't slip on the dance floor, but someone's spilt a drink there and as I step forward I skid and fall, throwing my hands out desperately for support. My outstretched hands hit the Yardie full in the chest and he goes down with me on top of him. As he falls, he swings the machete around and I feel something slice past my forehead, which is suddenly wet with some slick, warm liquid. He drops Toby, who scampers off the dance floor into the arms of his sobbing mother, who is crawling towards us across the sand. I cling to the bad guy, too scared to move, sick with fear and adrenaline, not knowing what to do next.

Behind me there's a great roar and I manage to turn my head for a second to see Mick running towards us, holding a chair over his head, which he throws towards the gang members standing on the dance floor. Claire is hard on his heels, screaming with thirty years of ugly bovine rage, a broken wine bottle in one hand. She looks like she's done this before. Trevor the teacher is still sitting in his seat, looking on with a curiously detached air, as behind him a dozen or more large, bearded Scandinavians decide this is not the time for neutrality.

Mick slams into one of the Yardies, bringing him crashing down next to where I am lying on top of their leader, who is dazed but awake and starting to struggle to get free from under me, pushing me away and wriggling towards the edge of the floor, where I can see he has dropped the machete. I grab his arms and hang on for dear life, not daring to think who he will carve up first if he gets his hands on it. Claire comes pounding onto the dance floor and lunges towards another of the gang with the broken bottle. He sidesteps her and swings a baseball bat into the back of her head. She staggers forward a few steps, her eyes rolling heavenwards, and crashes down on top of the Yardie leader, who has reached the edge of the dance floor, dragging me whimpering with him. I hear a distinctive crack and he jerks once, then lies completely still. Claire's full weight has landed across his neck on the edge of the raised floor, forcing his head backwards and sideways towards the sand some twelve inches below. She groans and rolls away, and then there is a rush of heavy, pounding feet as Sven and Olaf and Jerker the Berserker lead the Viking charge, a brief clash of improvised weapons and the Yardies break and flee.

Something sticky is covering my face as I lie on top of the Yardie leader, sick with fear, and black out.

◆ ◆ ◆

I am a hero.

I am in a private room in a hospital in Kingston, where a police guard and a member of the consular staff from the British High Commission are keeping the press at bay, while I am stitched up and have the chance to recover. Scattered around my room are press reports from the Jamaican and British press:

Banker Kills Yardie Thug
British Tourist Fights off Yardie Gang, Saves Toddler

and in the *Daily Post*,

Bulldogs: 1, Yardies: 0

There are flowers in my room from Mick and Claire, who were the first people allowed to visit me, Claire with a heavily bandaged head, along with Jason and Kennie, who declare me both 'cool' and 'wicked'.

There are flowers too from Sally and Trevor, who visited me briefly – he obviously had not been to a hospital before – and who brought with them Toby, Jasper and Monty, who had made me get well cards with felt tip pens and crayons, and asked how many stitches I'd had in my forehead, and would it leave a scar. Sally held my hand, and I squeezed hers, but luckily there was no chance to say any of the things that were swimming around in my head, like the fact that I did it for her, and was there any chance of a blow-job?

I've had a phone message from Wendy, who had no idea I was over here until she heard my name on the radio and read what had happened in the papers. She's offering to fly over and talk. Talk? Who's she kidding?

More promisingly, Dan Harriman sent a couple of hookers round dressed as nurses, but the Jamaican policeman on the door was nobody's fool and ordered them away. Good old Dan – at least he tried.

I've had lots of messages from people in the City, including some of my old team at Bartons, who seem baffled by what's happened. In fact, the common theme among everyone who knows me seems to be sheer bewilderment at what on earth got into me.

I can't think about what actually happened without needing to throw up. I still feel sick with fear, which the doctors, who clearly admire me enormously, are putting down to concussion. They tell me gravely that I will have a prominent scar across my forehead, that it may fade somewhat over time, but only plastic surgery can hope to reduce this savage mark. It is a high price to pay for courage, but it was only a fraction of an inch from slicing through my skull. They assure me that a machete blow that connected firmly to the head would have caused unthinkable consequences. I agree. I can't think about them either.

I'm still not taking phone calls – claiming headaches – and the doctors won't allow the press to talk to me, so Mick and Sally are the people who get to tell the story. When I see them interviewed on the cable television in my room, I wonder if they are talking about the same incident, or if they are, how much they had had to drink. It seems I not only charged the Yardie leader holding Toby, knocking him to the ground and wrestling with him, but in a desperate life and death struggle fought him to the bitter end, all the while bleeding copiously from the machete wound that had split my head open. When the Yardies fled, they left their leader dead on the edge of the dance floor with a broken neck, with me lying unconscious on top of him, weakened by loss of blood, but still clinging to him desperately. The news coverage includes photographs of me being helped from the scene, my face and my white Armani shirt soaked in blood, still looking shocked.

I can't quite believe it, but the story's all over the media, so it must be true.

My only bad moment comes when a superintendent from the Jamaican police comes to call. He is respectful, almost wary in my presence. First, he assures me that I'm not going to be charged with anything.

Charged? I almost leap out of bed and grab him, so that I can scream at him that I don't need to be charged because I didn't do anything.

But he goes on to say that there will be a coroner's enquiry, much as there would be in the UK, and that he believes the coroner will return a verdict of lawful killing. I can swear a deposition now and with luck, it will not be necessary for me to return for the hearing, although men like me are always welcome in Jamaica.

Men like me? This man knows nothing. I made three New Year resolutions this year: screw more beautiful women, smoke more cigars, and try to be more shallow. Okay, I'm joking about that last one. Oh, and get a bigger bonus, but that goes without saying. And now he thinks I'm a hero. He tells me that it's rare for tourists to make a stand as the guests of the Bay Club did that night. Tourists generally just panic and scream and hand over their valuables. I nod. Makes sense to me. But he tells me that I inspired them. A number of guests have said that when they saw me take the leader down, they thought they'd have a go.

Then he gets to the bad part. He tells me the Yardies are a dangerous group to cross. The man I killed (that's right – I killed) was a well-known gangland figure over here, and they have connections in London, where they play a major role in the drugs trade. I may feel I can look after myself, but I should still take 'sensible precautions'. Sensible precautions? I'm a man who thought sensible precautions meant wearing a condom. He totally freaks me out, and when he's gone, I cling to the bedcovers, pale and trembling.

♦ ♦ ♦

On the flight home, I get VIP treatment. I could get used to this. It's actually even better than Rory would get. The Minister of Tourism escorts me out to the plane, bypassing formalities and taking me directly airside. He shakes my hand,

and promises me a warm welcome and a more peaceful stay next time I come to Jamaica. I ignore the photographers, because I've got used to them by now, and anyway they're only the locals. Once I'm on board, back in seat 1A, the cabin crew can't do enough for me, and the other passengers look at me with awe. They know. One of them, an American business type, comes over and shakes my hand.

'I was a marine. Two tours in 'Nam. But I never did anything like you just did. Sir, it's a privilege to shake your hand.'

At Heathrow, there are more photographers, wanting to get a close-up of my battle scar, and some reporters wanting a quote about how good it feels to be home again. The airline has laid on a couple of people from Special Services, who escort me through to immigration. It's only when I'm in a taxi heading home that I begin to take stock and think what on earth I'm going to do next.

There's a pile of unopened mail in the flat. Lots of kind notes from well-wishers, messages on the answer-phone… and a letter from Rory:

'Dear Dave,

First, let me welcome you home and congratulate you on your very courageous act in Jamaica'.

Act? How does he know it was an act? How could he?

'I hope you are fully rested and well on the way to recovery, and that you will forgive me for raising a delicate business matter with you so soon after your return.
As you know, before your departure, we were discussing the difficulties of accommodating your full potential within the firm, and I think we had both agreed that it was time for you to move on.'

The shit. I'm a hero and he's firing me. How's that going to look in the press, Rory? But there's more.

> 'As part of the general restructuring plan currently being implemented at Barton's, we are in a position to offer you exceptionally generous terms if you are still of the view that it is best to seek fresh opportunities elsewhere.
> At a minimum we would be looking at granting you three years' total compensation, based on the average of your three highest earning years in the past five – approximately £2.5 million – as well as the immediate vesting of your options and employee shares. We would give you a very favourable reference, and be pleased to continue paying your basic salary and benefits until the earlier of twelve months or until you find suitable employment elsewhere.
> We would, however, naturally seek your agreement in writing that this concluded matters between us on a positive and final note, and that as a good leaver you bore no ill-will towards the bank or any of its employees.'

I can't believe it. He's paying me off. He's paying me off because he's frightened. He's offering to spend millions of the bank's money so that he doesn't have to worry about waking up one night to find me standing by his bed with a machete in my hand.

On reflection, it makes good sense. It's not his money he's offering me. And he's running scared. More than scared - he's read the papers. He knows I'm a killer.

There's also a letter from Wendy. She and Samantha are staying with her mother in Buckinghamshire, and she's had a lot of time to think. She acknowledges faults on both sides, and wants to 'try again'. We've both made mistakes – like running off with the personal trainer, though she doesn't say this – and after all I've been through I probably need a period of stability in my life. Could she have got wind of Rory's letter? There's nothing like a few million pounds to bring a woman round.

I put both letters down and call Dan Harriman. He's delighted I'm back, insists we have to celebrate and suggests we meet for drinks.

The best dry martinis in London are served at Duke's of St James's, a small boutique hotel beloved of Americans (who know a thing or two about cocktails) and sadly these days, hedge fund managers. The barmen here say that dry martinis are like women's breasts: two are too few and three are too many. As far as breasts go, I've always preferred four myself, in two pairs, both at the same time, but that's another matter.

We are soon on number three, and Dan is starting to slur his words.

'So you're leaving Bartons?'

I nod. 'Need another challenge.'

'Did they fire you?'

'Course not. But I've had it with being Rory's poodle.'

'Never bothered you before.'

I very gingerly finger the stitches on my forehead. I've developed a nervous tic in my cheek, which gets worse when I'm stressed, lying, or otherwise under pressure, which I'm finding is quite a lot of the time, and I can feel it now. Whenever it starts in my cheek, a pulse becomes visible on the side of my forehead where the scar is most prominent. I feel as if people can read me like a book. 'That was then. This is now.'

Dan nods, unconvinced. 'So where will you go?'

'No idea. Not a US firm – they work too hard. Not one of the old British firms either – too sleepy. Maybe I should start my own firm? Could you see me running somewhere? I quite fancy it. Maybe it's time.'

'Yeah, right. If I were you I'd get my arse back to Bartons in double quick time. Failing that, it's a sayonara job.'

'A sayonara job?'

He nods firmly. Sayonara jobs are the last jobs taken by struggling has-been's desperately clinging on to the City lifestyle, normally after a couple of divorces and a few years of the downward spiral at a proper firm. 'If you're not careful, you'll be head of capital markets at the Korean Farmers' Bank, running a department that comprises yourself and your assistant.'

I'm tempted to tell him about Rory's letter, but I don't. I need to get it finalised first, and whatever happens I need to get more. I know he won't see me, that I'll have to go back to him through Human Resources, who must be baffled by his decision. But if I don't squeeze another half a million out of him my name's not Dave Hart. I raise my glass to Dan.

'Who cares? Here's to the Korean Farmers' Bank, London Capital Markets Department. I'm an undemanding sort of guy. As long as I have a six-figure salary and an expense account, I'll be happy.'

I'm actually quite troubled. Dan could be right. However much I squeeze out of Bartons, I'll burn through it in no time, or if I don't, Wendy will – and then what will I do? The thing about friends is that they tell it to you straight. Dan and I will always be friends. We both know too much not to be.

Dan drains his glass. 'No more for me – I've got a seven o'clock flight tomorrow morning. Fancy a Chinese or an Indian on the way home?'

I shake my head. 'Nah. I think I'll go for a Ukrainian, or maybe a couple of Brazilians.'

It is only much later, when the girls have gone, and I'm alone again in the flat, that I get round to playing the answer-phone messages. I delete a couple from Wendy, and then come to one from a head-hunter.

'Mister Hart, my name is Susannah Grainger. I work for McLintey Dobbs, the executive search firm. We haven't met before, but you come highly recommended, and I wonder if you might be able to help us with an assignment we're working on. I'd be very grateful for your advice on a search we're conducting for someone who can run the London-headquartered investment banking operations of a major Continental European banking group. I'll try you again tomorrow, or if you have a moment, perhaps you'd be kind enough to call me on…'

I scribble the number down. Head-hunters always ask for 'advice', when they are really asking if you're interested. Am I interested? Hell, yes.

◆ ◆ ◆

Large, slow-moving Continental European banks with huge wedges of capital but small or non-existent investment banking operations, are like dinosaurs: too much weight and not enough brainpower to turn it around. They typically have highly profitable domestic franchises, based around hard-working citizens who save lots of money and demand little interest when they feed it into the branch network. They also tend to have large stakes in industrial companies dating back decades, often valued at nowhere near the current market price. Their board members see themselves as guarding the legacy of the past, unadventurous types who pay themselves little and take pride in offering their employees a job for life. Their businesses are both profitable and secure, if a little conservative.

Clearly, what these people need is me.

I'm sitting in the offices of McLinty Dobbs in St James's Square, sipping a cup of coffee and reading the annual report and accounts of EFG Bank – Erste Frankfurter Grossbank, one of the heavyweights of the German banking sector. Grossbank in German is a generic term meaning major bank, and these guys were the first one set up in Frankfurt – hence 'Erste Frankfurter'. Luckily someone round there spoke enough English to realise that answering the phone as First Frankfurter doesn't make a lot of sense, so instead they wisely chose to be known simply as Grossbank. Damned clever, these Germans. They only have a tiny London-based investment banking operation, but have recently appointed a new, and apparently thrusting, Chairman. Susannah Grainger is sitting opposite me with one of her colleagues, looking at a printout of my CV, which I e-mailed before the meeting. She's mid-forties, very thin, adequately dressed in a business suit that does little for her, and which I don't recognise, and has no interesting jewellery. I guess she can't be doing that well.

'The new chairman, Herman Schwartz, why does he think I'd be suitable? We've never met. He wouldn't know me from Adam.'

Susannah looks up from my CV. 'To be absolutely honest, I think it's what you did in Jamaica that caught his eye. You got a lot of coverage in the German press, you know. There were apparently some vivid eyewitness accounts of what happened from some of the German guests staying at the hotel.' Eyewitnesses? Shit. My cheek starts twitching. But she looks at me respectfully, as you would someone who has charged a gang of armed thugs, saved a little boy and killed their leader in single combat.

These days, people fortunate enough to be born in the Western world rarely encounter deadly violence. We have to suffer petty crime, and a very few of us might choose to serve in the armed forces, and be sent to dangerous places, but for most of us killing is something we hear about on the news or watch at the cinema.

That's why I'm exceptional.

'I see. And did you… check with Rory, as I suggested?'

'Yes. He confirmed the circumstances of your departure, the fact that you need a broader canvas – that was how he put it – and said very complimentary things about you. He was very helpful, and it's wonderful that someone so senior should make himself available at such short notice. I have to say, though, that he came across as rather nervous. I wonder if he thinks he's made a big mistake allowing you to leave Bartons.'

I can't help smiling. 'Oh, I don't know. How many alpha males can you get in the same room? I think if we're honest it's best for both of us to put some space between us.'

She nods. 'When I questioned him, he said something very similar himself.'

I sit back and smile. 'So when do I go to Frankfurt?'

♦ ♦ ♦

The new Grossbank tower is a landmark on the Frankfurt skyline. I'm whisked into town from the airport in a dark grey S-class Mercedes with a uniformed chauffeur, straight into the underground car park, where the head of personnel is waiting to greet me and take me to the fifty-fourth floor. Two very dour, Brünnhilde-like receptionists – definitely unfuckable, built like wardrobes - give me the once-over, and ask in guttural Germanic accents if I want the bathroom ('No, thank you, I had a shower before take-off'). Then I'm shown into a high-tech conference room with the most staggering view, that surely ought to be used as a film set for the next Bond movie.

Eleven elderly retired bank manager types are sitting around the conference table, staring at me with suspicion and perhaps a little nervousness, as if I've come to steal their wallets. I have. I want to say, 'Relax, guys, I'm the one being interviewed', but I know it would be wrong. Instead I stand at the end of the table, incline my head slightly towards them, just stop myself from clicking my heels and say, 'Good morning, gentlemen.' A few of them – presumably the ones who are not yet dead - incline their heads slightly in my direction, and one or two mutter 'Guten Morgen'. My hand-made silk suit probably cost more than all of theirs combined, and I feel for a moment conspicuously overdressed, but then I remember that they are hiring me to be an investment banker, and it's better that I look the part.

I'm about to sit down, when the doors behind me burst open, and a younger,

much more vigorous man in a half-way decent suit strides in. I recognise him as Herman Schwartz – 'Herman the German' – and I'm relieved to see that he's actually wearing an Hermès tie. He pumps my hands vigorously, looking sleek and elegant with his dark, carefully trimmed hair, his perma-tan complexion and his neat, slim figure. I know that he's forty-nine years old, and the youngest Chairman in the Bank's history, but he doesn't look a day over forty.

'Dave – may I call you Dave? – welcome to Frankfurt. We're very excited to meet you, aren't we, gentlemen?'

He looks to his colleagues for agreement, and most nod, though a few could easily be asleep, and some possibly don't understand English.

We sit down, he introduces his colleagues while coffee is served, and then the formal part begins.

Much of it is standard stuff. While I never really thought I'd be in this kind of situation, I'm a fast learner and I quickly identify their hot buttons. One key point is that they want me to tell them how they are perceived in the market. They are seeking a candid opinion, so I nod gravely and pause to reflect before replying. This stuff is so easy, just like pitching to a client. I've been doing it for years and even in my sleep I could lie for England.

'A sleeping giant.' In other words, fat, dumb and happy. 'Grossbank is hugely well capitalised, the only triple-A rated bank left in Germany.' Let me loose here and I'll soon change that. 'But it's never realised its full potential. It's never stretched itself outside its domestic market.' It's just stuck to solid, profitable business that it knows and understands. We'll soon change that as well. 'To the outside world, it's incredible that a bank of this size, of this historic importance, should be a lion at home and frankly a mouse overseas, especially when inter-national markets represent the best growth potential going forward. Standing still is not an option. We have to take this firm forward.' Forward and down-ward in the next great recycling operation of dumb foreign money in the City of London.

'But can we succeed?' It's one of the grey men, and I need to be careful because I actually thought he was asleep.

'With respect, that's the wrong question. We must succeed. It's not *if*, but *how*. Failure is not a possibility!' I bang my fist down on the table as I say this, and right on cue my face starts twitching. They all perk up and pay attention, and several of them, including Schwartz himself, start nodding their heads vigorously. I sometimes feel sorry for the older generation of Germans. It's hard for them to show true aggression without feeling guilty about their country's past and coming over all anxious that people will think they're going off to invade small nations again. But as a foreigner, albeit a potentially soon-to-be-hired gun, I have no such inhibitions. 'Gentlemen – the bank already has a presence in the London market, but it's neither one thing nor the other. Too big to be a niche player, and too small to go head-to-head with the big boys. It's forwards or die. I have a clear vision for what can be achieved in the London market. The only question is whether we have the will to deliver!'

I go off into a rant about how I've identified the ten major business areas that the bank should focus on, and how we will become a top three player in all of them within three years. We will swoop on other firms, hiring their best teams, paying premium rates for the best people in each business area, then let them loose with the full balance-sheet of the bank behind them. We'll take bigger positions, place bigger bets, and unleash the full unrealised potential of the most talented people in the market. Resistance is futile. Victory is inevitable.

Quite whether I could actually do any of this is another thing. As a mid-ranking, relatively low-flying MD at Bartons, no-one ever trusted me to try. And why should they? Only arch politicians like Rory got to play with the full train-set.

'What would you need in order to succeed?' This from Herman the German. All eyes are on me now.

'Carte blanche to hire and fire in your London operation as I see fit. Overall authority for running the investment banking business globally, including those parts of it that are located here in Frankfurt. In principle, agreement on the broad thrust of the product by product approach that I've just described and direct budgetary authority to implement it – and gentlemen, I'm assuming we'll invest a billion euros in the first year, and we'll be underwater for the first three years of operations. That's how long we'll need before the full potential of the huge money machine we're building can be released.' And I'll have left by then, having passed Go three times and collected the kind of money that would make Rory turn green.

'And what would you seek personally, always assuming you were successful?' This comes from one of the oldest board members present, someone not yet carried along by Herman's enthusiasm.

'Do you mean my own package?' He nods and glances at some of his colleagues. 'My own package would be huge.' He gives them an 'I told you so' look. 'It has to be. None of the top professionals we'd be looking to hire would take the career risk of joining a relatively unknown name without significant upside. And in investment banking, you lead from the top. People expect their bosses to be high earners.' I briefly catch Herman's eye. This is clearly music to his ears, not that he would ever put his personal interests before those of the bank, obviously. I shrug carelessly. 'I don't care about the detail, only the big picture. It has to be convincing, gentlemen – the going rate and then some.' For once I'm relieved that my cheek doesn't start twitching.

◆ ◆ ◆

My first Christmas alone since I got married passes in an alcohol and drug fuelled haze of heaving, panting, naked bodies. Did I say drugs? What I meant to say is that there were a lot of parties where certain people were doing drugs. I admit I occasionally have a glass too many of falling over juice, and I have from time to time been partial to the fairer sex, but drugs are not my scene. Honestly.

As a newly single man, with a bank balance freshly fattened for Christmas by Rory's generosity – I got him up to three million, to the amazement of Bartons' HR department – and Wendy still camping out in Buckinghamshire with Samantha, I had a ball. In fact, several balls, often on the same night.

Wendy doesn't know about the settlement with Bartons, for which I opened a new bank account, and I have to be careful not to create the wrong impression, but recklessly I decided to send Samantha a last minute surprise: half the toy department at Harrods, knowing that Wendy's mother lives in a tiny cottage where it would be impossible to unpack, let alone play with, a full-sized Wendy house, a Cinderella castle, giant-sized cuddly toys of all the Disney characters, nine different dressing-up outfits, and two new tricycles.

I sent Wendy nothing.

She called on Christmas morning, but I cut her off before she could say a word. 'Don't say a thing. Don't expect me to apologise, don't expect any regrets. Anything I may have done I did because you drove me to it. You pushed me over the edge, and now here we are. Before you complain, before you accuse, think about it.'

Then I hung up dramatically and ignored it when the phone kept ringing, partly because I thought it was the right thing to do, and partly because I was too busy with Tygra, nineteen, from Estonia, and Charlotte, twenty-one, from Lithuania, for whom I had bought presents.

Like all good things, it came to an end, and in the first week of January I started work at Grossbank, on a package of 'three by five' – a five-million pound a year bonus, guaranteed for three years - with the same again in employee stock, plus a million sign-on (i.e., they pay me a million pounds just for turning up on the first day) and a further ten-million pound package of stock that vests in five years if I'm still around and achieve certain pretty astronomical revenue targets (I very cleverly hung out for this, because it made them think I might be here for the long term – as if…) I'm counting on Wendy not reading the financial press, because there are some inconvenient reports that I wouldn't want her to see:

> *Grossbank are rumoured to be paying top dollar for City hard man and former Bartons investment banker Dave Hart, who last year hit the headlines when he took on Yardie gangsters in Jamaica, killing their leader and rescuing British toddler Toby Mills.*
> *Hart, who still sports a prominent scar from a machete wound, was unavailable for comment…*

That's it, I have my label now. I'm 'City hard man' – me! I've been defined. In any event, I need a disguise to wear to work at the new firm, and City hard man seems fair enough, at least for people who don't know me. So I summon up my full chameleon-like capabilities and morph into a City hard man – or at least what I think a real City hard man might be like, if ever there were such a thing.

It doesn't help that it's January, when most of the City goes dry. After the pre-Christmas excesses, bodies saturated with alcohol are drying out. This is when people briefly start going to the gym, try to lose a few pounds, and generally get serious. Where before they might have gone out at lunchtime, now they stay at their workstations. Where before they met for drinks after work, now they return home, miserable, unfulfilled, full of suppressed rage.

And the markets roar. Analysts talk about the January effect in the stock market, referring to the way in which share prices soar – and sometimes plunge – amid heavy volumes of aggressive trading. Theses have been written about why it happens, but behind closed doors we know. Fifty thousand market makers, traders, sales traders, dealers and brokers are drying out. And they're like a whole herd of buffalo with sore heads.

That's the backdrop when I arrive at the Grossbank London office on my first Monday morning.

Grossbank are in a small building off Threadneedle Street, not far from the Bank of England, but a million miles from the giant concrete and glass palaces of Bartons and the other major firms. A few hundred people work here, but until now I've never even met someone from Grossbank London, let alone known anyone – they were just too far down the food chain.

Sometimes new bosses like to make an impression by arriving at the crack of dawn, catching everyone unprepared, and then proceed to install a new regime of early morning meetings to show how macho they are. For their first month, they don't leave the office until late into the evening, forcing everyone else to stay at their workstations. And they appear in the office at weekends, checking on who's working.

As a fundamentally lazy person, I think that's all bullshit.

I arrive just before ten, by which time they are wondering if something's happened to me. I have a newly prepared corner office made by combining the offices of the head of equities and the head of research – who are now sitting in much smaller offices next to the trading floor, scowling at me. I make a note to fire them.

I have been given a long-serving secretary, mid-forties, half-German, unmarried, and built like a barn door. Her name is Maria, and she has been with Grossbank in London and Frankfurt for nearly twenty years. She's definitely a spy, put here to keep an eye on me, and I immediately decide I have to keep her.

That's right, I'm going to keep her. Keep her, and use her. She'll be my back door communication channel to the board. I spend the first day going through formalities, getting my photograph taken, signing endless papers, and meeting the faceless, one-dimensional people who served the old regime.

By four o'clock, having eaten nothing more than a sandwich at my desk, feeling the desperate need for alcohol, and with my face twitching at a medium fast rate, I'm overcome by the desire to do something. You know what they say. Lonely? Bored? Depressed? Call a meeting! I call a meeting.

My meeting takes place in the conference room next to my office. Maria summons for me the heads of equities, fixed income, treasury, foreign exchange and structured finance. I ask where the head of corporate finance is, but am reminded that we don't actually do corporate finance. Oh.

I find myself staring around the table at a group of nervous, defensive verging on hostile, fifty-something men. So this is where they all go when they get moved on from proper firms. At Bartons only the Chairman and the people actually running the firm were over fifty. I realise then that the Grossbank London office was a sayonara job.

I get them each to give me five minutes on their business area, its achievements, strengths, weaknesses, and finally ask them to say who on their team they would rate as their star performer. I make notes, nod, twitch, but don't smile. When the last of them has finished, I pass a note to Maria, then while away the minutes in small talk, asking them how long they've all been at Grossbank, where they were before, do they have kids – or even grandchildren – and so on.

The London head of HR is in my office, summoned by Maria, and in another glass-sided conference room, visible to the heads of business areas sitting with me, another group is assembling – the individuals they named as their star performers, or at any rate the people in their departments who were the least bad.

'Excuse me, gentlemen – I'll be right back.' I leave the conference room and return to my office. The head of HR looks no different to the men I've just left – mid-fifties, tired, ragged round the edges, on the downward slope of a City career.

'I'm Dave Hart – what's your name?'

'Charles Butler, Mister Hart.'

'Call me Dave.' I point to the conference room I've just left. 'Charles, do you see those men in there?'

'Yes, Dave.'

'You know who they are?'

'Of course.'

'Good, because I'm firing everyone in the room. Call Security, have them send some people up to walk them out of the building. Tell your people to draw up severance papers.' I pat him on the arm and return to the conference room, where there is a sweaty odour of fear and a deathly hush.

I stand at the end of the table. 'Gentlemen, this place is a joke.' One or two of them frown and cross their arms, and there are a couple of muttered 'Steady on's'. I pause and stare around the table, waiting for absolute silence. 'I don't feel like I've come into an investment bank at all. I feel like I've walked onto the set of "Carry On Banking". Well let me assure you, there's a new era dawning at Grossbank.' They nod, trying to summon some enthusiasm, though probably feeling sick to their stomachs. 'An era of high performance, high ambition…' I hesitate before allowing myself to smile. '…and high pay.'

'Hear, hear!' It's the head of treasury, Norman something or other.

I pause and stare at him. 'Be quiet, you obsequious little shit.' My face is twitching, right on cue, and I stare at him.

'I… I'm sorry.'

'Quiet!' I slam my hand down hard on the table, then look slowly around the room. On the trading floor beyond the glass walls of the conference room people are looking at us, wondering what's going on. They know the men in this room. The men in this room run Grossbank London. They are Grossbank London. And now, as they look at me, they are truly frightened. This man kills. This Dave Hart, a man they'd never heard of until last year, a man who took out a gangster with his bare hands, now seems barely under control. They are fascinated by my twitching face, the scar, the manic spittle that flies whilst I talk.

'A new era is dawning, and you, gentlemen, will not be part of it.' I point at them each in turn. 'You, and you, and you, and you, and you, have failed. All of you. You had one of the greatest opportunities in investment banking in the City of London, and you blew it.' I look up to see several security guards standing outside with Charles Butler and a couple of his assistants. All activity has come to a stop on the trading floor. All eyes are on me, standing in this glass bubble with five – five – petrified victims in front of me. For years I took this shit. Now I'm dishing it out. Awesome. My voice is a hoarse whisper. 'You had the opportunity to build something great, with the strength, the muscle, of one of the world's most powerful financial institutions behind you. And you didn't even know it. You're all fired. Now get out of here!'

This job rocks.

As if one meeting in an afternoon isn't enough, I then walk over to the second conference room. The group sitting here are about ten to fifteen years younger than their bosses, one or two look quite keen and bright, but in general they strike me as classic big fishes in small, sleepy ponds. Only now there's a shark loose in their pond.

Once again, I position myself at the end of the table, standing looking down at them. 'Gentlemen, good afternoon. We haven't actually met, and if you'll excuse me, I'm not proposing to go through the usual round of introductions.' I look around the table with a sort of twisted half smile on my face. 'You see that room over there?' They nod and glance over to where I've come from, where a group of bitter, broken men are being led away to collect their personal belongings. 'I've just fired everyone in that room.' This brings a sharp intake of breath, tempered by a venal, self-interested glint in the eyes of one or two who think they see an opportunity. 'Some of you won't be around long enough to make it worthwhile investing the time in getting to know you. Those who make it will soon get to know me anyway. I'm placing each of you in temporary charge of your departments. If I don't see a material improvement in results over the next month, you'll be replaced. If you deliver, you can expect great things. Each of you will have a five minute slot with me each day to report how well you've done. Don't send me paper, don't send me e-mail – talk to me. And each day I'll be spending at least an hour walking round the office, dropping in from time to time, just to keep my finger on the pulse. You'll get used to it.'

I actually have no idea what their results are like. For all I know they might be stellar, though from the look of the previous heads of businesses I doubt it. Anyway, it was my first Monday. I was bored, and I hate January.

Two meetings in one day is quite enough. When I get back to my office I tell Maria to get me Herman on the phone.

'Herman? Hi, it's Dave. Great. First day's been terrific. We're making very significant progress already. I've just fired everyone.'

By five thirty I'm out of there, in a cab home, calling up Ilyana from Kiev and Natalia from Bucharest.

◆ ◆ ◆

Tuesday's financial press carries some interesting stories. The best headline reads *Bloodbath at Grossbank*. I wonder what Rory will make of that one. They're all running the line that 'City hard man' Dave Hart marked his first day in his new job by firing all the heads of department in what was clearly a carefully orchestrated plan. The tiny quarter page devoted to business news in the *Daily Post* is the one I like best: *Hart by Name, Hard by Nature*.

But now the heat's on and I need to move fast.

When I get to the office, somewhere around nine-thirty, I call another meeting. Maria's already finding it hard to get people to come to meetings with me, but I insist that they drop whatever they were doing and attend. The first meeting is with Bill Foreman, who is nominally in charge of marketing and PR for the London operation. I say 'nominally', because before I came here, people had barely heard of Grossbank London.

He's a lean, nervous type in his mid-thirties, wearing a collarless shirt buttoned up to the top and no tie. Probably thinks it's media-cool. He worked for a succession of minor PR agencies before winding up at Grossbank five years ago.

When he first enters my office, I'm sitting in my big leather power-chair, staring out the window. He stands awkwardly, coughs, and then falls silent, waiting for me to acknowledge him. He probably thinks it's a power game, but the reality is that Ilyana and Natalia gave me simply the best time ever last night. I don't know what we were all on – well, I do, but I'm not telling you – but we carried on until four, and I'm honestly feeling pretty shagged out, as well as hung over – and yes, I know it's January, but anyone can slip momentarily. I've got shadows under my eyes and I feel as if I'm labouring just that little bit harder against gravity today – it's a 2G day. With a monumental effort I swing my chair around and stare at him. I have only a mild twitch, probably due to tiredness rather than stress. He remains standing, awkwardly, and I don't signal him to sit down.

'Bill, our PR is crap.'

'I – I agree.'

'You agree?' I'm taken aback by his candour.

'Of course. It's all directed from Frankfurt, and they have no idea how the British press works. Their marketing campaigns are crass and heavy-handed, and they never want to spend any money.'

'Oh.' I gesture to the chair beside him, the strategically low, deep chair that leaves even the tallest visitor looking up at me, either hunched forward with their feet on the ground, or sitting right back with their legs dangling. He chooses to hunch, cravenly I feel, probably anticipating a summary execution.

Perhaps he senses my hesitation, and like a Death Row inmate holding out for a governor's pardon, he'll say anything to secure a delay in the sentence. 'Have you ever seen the posters they wanted us to put up? The huge ones to go on billboards in the City, and as full page ads in the financial press? *If size matters to you, choose Grossbank* – can you imagine? We'd have been a laughing stock. Then they had *Grossbankers make sure our clients come first and we come second* – they'd commissioned all this from a German agency that had never done any work in the UK. It was all I could do not to use this stuff.'

Remarkable. A head of marketing and PR, who spends his time avoiding marketing. But I can see what he means.

'Bill – which is the most expensive, trendy, high profile PR firm in the UK?'

'Ball Taittinger.'

'Get them in here. I want to meet them to discuss a marketing campaign for Grossbank London.'

'You bet. Fantastic. It's what I've wanted to do for years.' He looks as if a huge weight has been lifted from his shoulders.

'Bill?'

'Yes, Mister Hart?'

'Call me Dave. Bill – congratulations!'

'Wh… what do you mean?'

'You've just survived a meeting with me. You see, it is possible.'

He laughs, thinking I'm joking, but when I don't respond he dries up.

'Thank you, Bill.'

He tries to stutter something, nods and exits.

Next on is Charles Butler, the head of HR. I've got in front of me the bonus list for last year.

'Charles, these bonuses were a disgrace.'

'Wh – what do you mean, Dave?'

'I mean how can people live, when they get paid like this, let alone perform out there in the market?'

'I – I don't see your point. Last year was a pretty reasonable year by Grossbank standards.'

'But the biggest bonus paid, presumably to one of our "star performers", was three hundred and fifty thousand pounds. Charles, how can a man live on that sort of money? Don't our people have wives and children and homes and yachts and fast cars? Don't they have dreams and aspirations, mistresses and drug habits?'

He's not sure how to take this last point, and smiles and nods – just the way I did with Rory! – as if he's getting used to my slightly zany sense of humour. 'But Dave – the firm can only pay what it produces. We're not very profitable.'

It's true. The whole London office produced less last year than the worst performing business area at Bartons – mine, as it happens – so they couldn't pay out.

'Charles, all this is going to change. We're going to implement Plan Alpha.'

'Plan Alpha?'

I nod. 'Plan Alpha. It's what I discussed with the board in Frankfurt.' They didn't actually know it as Plan Alpha, and neither did I until a few seconds ago, but it's all I can manage when I feel like this. I get up and walk over to a flip chart. 'Charles – you know the management structure we've employed in the past in London?'

'Of course. Matrix reporting. Business heads reported in functionally to Frankfurt, and each region had its "champion" on the board, with geographic responsibility.'

I pause. I didn't know that. It sounds pretty sensible to me. But it's such an effort to stand here concealing my hangover, that I press on anyway.

'We're going to adopt a new structure.' I pick up a red marker pen and draw a square box on the flip chart. Inside the box I write 'Me'. 'Okay, Charles, let's take this slowly. Here I am. Are you with me so far?'

He nods, giving me an uncertain, sideways look. I then draw two diagonal lines stretching downwards and outwards from the first box. I draw two more boxes and write in one, 'Head of Markets', and in the other 'Head of Corporate'. I turn back to Charles.

'This is the new structure. Simple, lean, streamlined, easy to understand and manage.' I point at the two boxes. 'The head of markets runs equities, fixed income, treasury, foreign exchange, and the head of corporate runs all the corporate client facing businesses – structured finance, corporate lending, project finance, new business areas we don't yet have a presence in, like mergers and

acquisitions, leasing and capital raising. The underlying businesses report in to them. They make a whole raft of strategic hires, bring in complete teams from other firms, and take responsibility for their businesses and their results.'

'So what do you do?'

'I'm in charge of the two of them.'

He seems puzzled, as if he doesn't quite get it. 'But I thought you…'

I cut him off. I don't have time to waste. 'Charles, I'm going to need the best headhunters in the business ready and raring to go when these people come on board. We'll be hiring people like they're going out of fashion.'

He points to the two boxes I've just drawn. 'B – but do you know who these people are?'

'Sure. I'm planning to recruit both of them this week.'

♦ ♦ ♦

It's Friday morning, and I'm having breakfast at Claridge's with Paul Ryan, the Chief Operating Officer at Hardman Stoney. A few weeks ago, Paul wouldn't even have taken my call, but now he's positively deferential.

In fact they all are. Just in the past few days I've had breakfasts, lunches and dinners with a bunch of people who would never previously have given me the time of day. Some of them tell me they checked me out with Rory, who was unusually reticent and if he did say anything, limited his advice to telling them to 'be careful'. The kind of people I'm talking about are all in the 'three million and over' club – that's annual bonus, in case you were wondering. They're successful, wealthy people accustomed to dealing at the top table.

And I wouldn't hire any of them.

The reason I'm having breakfast with Paul is that he's different. The others I wanted to meet because I needed a crash course in top table manners and conduct – the way they speak, the way they relate to one another, the things they think about. Pretty soon I'll find myself in a situation outside the safe haven of Grossbank's London office, and I'll have to act the part. The Emperor might be stark naked, but there's nothing to be gained from advertising the fact.

And if I'm honest, I got an ever so tiny thrill from having Maria call these people up and invite them out, at very short notice, so I could listen to what they had to say while scarcely opening my mouth, and then not offer them a job. It spooks them, when nothing happens, and it creases me up.

Paul on the other hand is quiet, serious, understated, and very practical. He's six-foot three, with a lean, athletic build, wavy dark hair, film star good looks, a neat, perfectly trimmed appearance, and a penchant for wearing sunglasses throughout the year. Naturally, being so good looking and well turned out, he's gay. The reason he's COO of one of the biggest and most aggressive US firms is that he gets things done. Senior investment bankers can generally talk a good story – at least by the time they reach board level - but they're not good at doing things.

Paul knows his business inside out. He designed the software programmes that the firm runs on, and he's a master of the detail that sends me to sleep but keeps a business running: information and reporting systems, risk management, IT.

'Don't you get sick of being COO?'

'Why should I? I'm irreplaceable, no-one wants my job, and I get very well paid. I keep my head down, stay out of the politics, and don't get hurt when the market falls out of bed or rates go haywire.'

'But is this it? Is this as far as you go?'

'What else is there?'

'How old are you?'

'Forty-one.'

'Forty-one? That's crazy. You can't stop now. You can't just… hang up your ambition and say "that's it, I'm going to sit here and get fat and happy".' Everyone needs a new challenge.'

'What sort of challenge?'

I lean forward across the table and try to put on my energised, enthusiastic, messianic look – though not too close, in case he gets a hint of my stale alcohol breath. I came here directly from an all night session with Barbara from Estonia and Nina from Columbia.

'Head of Markets at Grossbank.' I hold up my hand and start counting off businesses. 'Let me see – running equities, fixed income, treasury, FX, derivatives, commodities and precious metals…'

'But Grossbank isn't in half those businesses, and the ones you are in you come nowhere. You're talking fantasy investment banking.'

I lean back triumphantly. 'Exactly. Fantasy is the word. You inherit a bit here and a bit there – the legacy businesses – but in most areas you have a blank canvas. Build your own firm, in your own style, with your own ethos, your own systems, your own infrastructure. You've got three years and a billion euros to do it. Hire whoever you want. Hell, if you really want to, you could buy the opposition. It would still be small change for Grossbank. The only rule is that you must succeed.'

The thing about Paul is that he could really do this. He'd have the credibility, the experience, the technical expertise, to pull together a world class business. In fact he has everything that I don't have, which is why, like all good bosses, I want to delegate the real work to someone far brighter and more competent than myself. I want to say that the Panzer divisions are on the march, and you are either with us, or you can be crushed beneath our tracks, but Paul is too thoughtful for that kind of rhetoric. 'How many times in your one unrepeatable life is someone going to make you an offer like that?' I pass him a napkin. 'Here – write down what you want by way of a package.'

With my right hand taken care of, I need to sort out my left hand. Whoever I hire to be Head of Corporates needs to have a natural top table manner, great connections, smoothness, charm, but also steel. Of all the people I've come across, 'Two Livers' MacKay is the most outstanding candidate, different in a way that I find exciting, but which some find hard to take. Two Livers has a reputation as one of the hardest drinking corporate coverage officers in the City of London. Starting at Bartons, then moving on to Schleppenheim, and finally Berkmann Schliebowitz, Two Livers outdrank the Russians at vodka to win some of the great Russian privatisation mandates, out-Scotched the Koreans and Japanese to refinance both countries' heavy industries after their markets crashed, and out-Schnappsed the Germans to pull off the first hostile takeovers in what had been a closed corporate world. A lot of people are jealous of Two Livers – mostly people who missed out on mandates they thought were in the bag – and a lot, myself included, admire the ruthlessness, the single-minded determination, and the dedication of a true corporate stormtrooper. And there's one other thing about Two Livers. She's beautiful.

Two Livers MacKay is one of the new breed of women in the City who are good for something other than typing or shagging. She's thirty-six, single, blonde, with a great figure and an Olympic athlete of a liver. She needs very little sleep, works like a dog and looks like a goddess. I haven't spoken to her in almost ten years. In her early days at Bartons, we were pretty close for a moment – a brief coming together on a business trip to Madrid. But she sussed pretty quickly that I was a shallow, vacuous low-flyer who wasn't to be trusted and would never commit.

Now things are different. Now a random spin of the wheel on the great roulette table of the Square Mile means that I can offer her even more millions than she's getting at Berkmann Schliebowitz. Suddenly she wants to have dinner again.

I'm meeting her at Gordon Ramsay tonight, but first I have a chore to deal with – Wendy wants to meet me. She wants to know 'what it is that I want'. Typical woman's question – hell, I don't even know what I want, other than money and success and fine malt whisky and willing, nubile young things in my bed at night. I may be a hero in some people's eyes, a big swinging dick in others, but at heart I'm just a guy.

I go back to the flat and change into my oldest suit, undo my top button, loosen my tie and splash some whisky on my face like after-shave. Then I wander round the corner to the coffee bar – 'neutral ground' – where we've agreed to meet.

The first thing I notice is that she's made an effort. Starting with the shoes – Manolo Blahnik - up through the legs – freshly waxed, with a silky sheen and a tan – to the skirt and jacket – Chanel – and the yellow and white gold necklace and matching bracelet – Bulgari. She's at her elegant best. She looks like the kind of woman who would be an asset to any greedy, vain, ambitious investment banker.

Except that's not what I am any more.

I explain that I'm in bad shape. In desperation after being shafted by Rory in the bonus round at Bartons, I've taken my sayonara job at Grossbank. She knows as well as I do that Grossbank are a joke. It's not how I ever imagined I'd end up, but needs must, and now I have to do whatever I can to make ends meet. I fear that we've grown too far apart for a reconciliation, and besides, I never saw her with a loser. She deserves better, and she's still young enough and good-looking enough to try. Whatever we decide should be friendly, civilised, and involve as few lawyers as possible. Samantha should be the priority and we should put her interests first. And anyway, I'm having so much fun shagging hookers and snorting nose candy that I'd have to be an idiot to get back together with her.

Just kidding about that last bit.

The trouble is, Wendy's nobody's fool. She tells me she's heard from Gloria Finkelstein – wife of Matt Finkelstein, who runs the swaps desk at Hardman Stoney – that Grossbank have actually given me a real job, with power and authority and that I'm doing things like firing people and offering big packages to new hires. She wants to know what I'm earning because as the woman who stood by me all through the tough years of my early career, she surely has a right to some of the benefits now that I've re-launched myself?

I take her hand across the table and look her earnestly in the eye. I'm good at this. I assure her that I would never, ever wish to deceive her about any aspect of my career, my finances or my life. We've been together too long and know each other too well for that. I promise to get her a copy of my contract of employment from Grossbank to settle things between us once and for all. We agree to meet again in a few weeks' time. She asks if I'd like to see Samantha this weekend and I explain that I'd love to, but I've got urgent business to attend to in Lithuania and Estonia, and she gives me a parting peck on the cheek, wrinkling her nose when she realises that it's ten a.m. and I've already been on the whisky.

After she leaves, I head back to the flat again, wash and change, and take a cab to the office. I ask Maria to call Charles Butler in.

He appears about thirty seconds later, looking nervous, as if his time might finally have come.

'Good morning, Charles.' I don't look up and I don't smile, but my cheek is twitching.

'Good morning, Dave.'

I toss Paul Ryan's napkin across the desk. He stares at it, uncomprehending.

'Paul Ryan's leaving Hardman Stoney.'

'Really?' Charles looks as if he doesn't understand the significance of this. I wait a few seconds, and finally he asks, 'Where's he going?'

'He's coming here.'

'Here?' Charles almost laughs. 'Paul Ryan is coming here? What's he going to do?'

'This job.' Without looking over my shoulder I raise one hand to point to the right hand side of the flip chart behind me.

'What job?' Charles is looking puzzled.

I turn and see that my 'org chart' is gone, presumably removed by the cleaners – or maybe Maria, to be sent secretly to the board? - and I'm pointing at a blank sheet of paper. 'Plan Alpha. Head of Markets.'

'Oh.' Another pause. 'You mean *the* Paul Ryan?'

'No. I'm talking about the other Paul Ryan. The one who works in the mailroom at Hardman Stoney as a messenger. That's the one we're hiring.'

For an instant his eyes widen, but then he realises it's just my little joke and he finally rises to the occasion.

'Congratulations! That's amazing. People won't believe it. I can hardly believe it myself. It will finally give us credibility. I mean – even more credibility than we already have since you joined.'

I indicate the napkin on the desk. 'We worked his package out on a napkin, and shook hands on it over breakfast. Draw up an offer letter, would you?'

He picks up the napkin and examines it, frowning. 'What exactly am I looking for?'

I grab it back and look at it, turning it over several times in frustration. Damn, I've picked up the wrong one. That's what comes from doing important meetings when you've been shagging all night and you're still half cut.

'Maria!'

She appears at the door. 'Yes, Mister Hart?'

'Call Claridge's. See if they can find the other napkin from our table. Paul wrote some numbers on it. It's quite important.'

'Yes, Mister Hart.'

I no longer have any idea what numbers he wrote, other than that they were impressively large. Damn. I look at Charles and tap the side of my head.

'Need to fix my head. Sometimes think I'm going crazy.'

'Really?'

I don't reply, but rub my chin pensively. 'Charles, there's one other thing.'

'What's that, Dave?' He's watching me intently, and I think I can spot a nervous tic in his cheek too. I wonder if eventually everyone at Grossbank will have one.

'Charles, I don't know quite how to put this, so I'll tell it to you straight. I'm having to let you go.'

'G – go? G – go where?' He knows exactly what I mean, but is in denial.

'I didn't know how to do this, and to be frank, I'm not really sure how to fire the head of HR. After all, you're supposed to be the one who handles all the firings. And you can't exactly fire yourself, can you?' I smile benevolently and walk around the desk to stand behind him, a friendly hand on his shoulder.

'W – why?'

'Why? Well it's obvious, isn't it? You don't fit in.'

He half turns to face me. 'H – how?'

'You have no sense of humour. You don't laugh. You don't fit in.'

'But I try to. I really do.'

'Okay. Let me give you an example.' I start pacing round the room, so that he has to squirm and wriggle in the low chair to follow me. 'I'm planning a practical joke to play on some friends of mine. People I've known for a long time, and who have a great sense of fun. I want to show them a contract of employment, on official Grossbank letterhead, that shows me earning, oh… let's just say a preposterously small amount of money. At Bartons, I'd have gone to the head of HR, who would have run me off a contract in a flash, and would have asked me afterwards how it went. But you're distant, you have no sense of fun, you don't join in.'

He's nodding now, frantically, and almost trips over the words in his haste. 'I c-c-can do that. I think that would be terribly funny. A scream. You w-want a prop for a practical joke? Of course, no problem, we're great practical jokers here.'

'Really? I must have misjudged you. Okay, let's put it to the test.' I look at my watch. 'It's quarter to twelve. I have an important recruitment dinner tonight, and my back's been giving me such gyp that I'm seeing my acupuncturist at twelve-thirty, which means I'll probably work from home for the rest of the day. Let's see what you can do before I leave the office in, say twenty minutes, shall we?'

He nearly sprints from the room. What a good man. I can see that we're going to get along fine. My acupuncturist is nineteen years old, blonde and comes from Belarus. And after that I'll probably be so tired that I'll have to sleep until dinner.

♦ ♦ ♦

The Gordon Ramsay restaurant in Royal Hospital Road, Chelsea, provides the ultimate dining experience: sublime food served in perfect surroundings with exceptional wines and service that is attentive without being intrusive. There could be no better place to meet Laura 'Two Livers' MacKay. I get there ten minutes early, still feeling tired after extending my acupuncture session by three hours – some of these nineteen-year-olds have incredible stamina. I'm worried that I might fall asleep. The trouble is that Viagra extends my ability to perform way beyond what my body can naturally sustain. I'm not a marathon runner, just a regular guy who eats too much rich food, drinks too much and never exercises. I need to slow down. At this rate I could kill myself.

There are a smattering of diners at other tables, chatting quietly to the occasional tinkle of cutlery on plates and the chinking of glasses. It's peaceful, discreet, luxurious.

And then there's a hush.

I look up to see a vision of beauty drifting serenely across the room. She's wearing an elegant, pale yellow mid-length dress and matching shawl by Loro Piana. The dress is not particularly low-cut – too sophisticated for that – but it clings to her body as if she was sewn into it. She's got amber and gold earrings, beautifully crafted, and to my shame I can't place them. Around her neck she has a matching amber pendant. No rings on either hand, which is a relief.

I stand to greet her, beaming like a kid in a candy store. 'Two Livers – how the hell are you? It's been a while.'

She dazzles me with her perfect white smile, ignores my outstretched hand and leans close to kiss me on the cheek – not a formal peck, but a softly lingering kiss that allows me to soak in her perfume – *Un Bois Vanille* by Serge Lutens. As her cheek gently caresses mine, she whispers in my ear, 'Yes.'

YES? A voice in my head is screaming at me. What does she mean – yes? The maitre d' pulls the chair out for her and she sits down, leaving me feeling like an awkward teenager, way out of my depth and struggling for words. I sit down and bury myself in the formalities of what would she like to drink – a large Screwdriver made with Uluvka vodka – and does she prefer still or sparkling – neither – and would she like to look at the menu – no, she already knows what she wants.

'Yes.' She's leaning forward across the table, smiling, running her fingers up and down the tall cocktail glass that's just been placed in front of her. Her eyes are fixed on mine.

Damn. At my time of life, there aren't many women who can do this to me. I put down the menu, trying not to appear flustered. 'Yes?'

'Yes, I want to work for Grossbank – I'll need three by four sterling with a million sign-on and a buyout of my unvested paper – and yes, I'll have sex with you.' Her voice is low, husky and clear. And she definitely said she'd have sex with me.

I put the menu down. 'Great.' I look around to see if anyone else has heard our conversation. 'How hungry are you?'

She lifts her glass and I watch while she downs it in one. 'Not hungry at all. Shall we go?'

The problem with having sex with four different women in twenty-four hours, not getting any sleep, rushing around London in taxis to attend high impact recruitment meetings, seeing your soon-to-be-ex-wife, having to lie convincingly to her about the true state of your finances, and having to threaten your head of HR to get him to produce a bogus contract of employment that you can use to deceive said soon-to-be-ex-wife, is that the toll eventually catches up with you.

Just as Two Livers and I collapse naked onto the bed in my apartment, our clothes scattered on the carpet where we have pulled them off, I pass out. I wish it were otherwise, but the cumulative effect of all that's been going on finally hits me. When I eventually wake up, around six the next morning, she's gone. I wonder if any of it really happened, until I wander into the bathroom, and see written on the mirror in red lipstick: 'Yes. 3 x £4 + £1 sign-on + buyout. + sex.'

♦ ♦ ♦

Things are going well. We've fired a lot of people, mostly second-rate, and we've hired a bunch of first-rate people, all very expensive, and hardly any of them available to start for several months, because their spiteful firms are enforcing the gardening leave provisions in their contracts. Grossbank's London business has actually picked up slightly, as people make a real effort to avoid what they fear might be a campaign of ethnic cleansing once the new people start.

So why have I been summoned to Frankfurt? I call Herman and he sounds almost apologetic. 'It's Doktor Biedermann. He's one of the old guard. He doesn't like what he hears about the London operation. He used to be responsible for the London office on the board. He personally knew most of the former business heads. In fact he was responsible for hiring them.'

'So what does he want?'

'He wants to trip you up. He wants you to come to Frankfurt far too soon, before any of your efforts have born fruit, and be humiliated. It's the old way. It's his way.'

'And what do you suggest I do?'

'Come here and face him. You of all people are not a man to run away from confrontation.'

Damn. 'You bet, Herman. Let me know just as soon as I can come over.'

'Next Tuesday would be good. The regional managers from all over Germany will be here. You could address them first, and then talk to those board members who are… most concerned about our investment banking strategy.'

'Next Tuesday? Really? Great. That's… five days away. Wonderful – I'll see you Tuesday morning.'

Double damn. All investment bankers live in fear of being found out. This really could be it. This could be the moment when they say it was all a joke. Did I seriously think they'd put me in charge of anything, let alone running the entire London office? Being in charge is all about faking it. I like to think I can fake it with the best of them. But if you so much as blink you're dead. I could already feel the onset of rigor mortis.

'Maria!'

'Yes, Mister Hart?'

'Maria – get me the smartest associate in the firm. I need a presentation prepared on our global strategy – a complete business plan in fact. Budgets, revenue forecasts, the lot. And a speech. A killer speech for Frankfurt.'

She hesitates. I look at her, irritated. 'What's the problem?'

'Where will he get the information? I don't think we have any budgets or forecasts or plans.'

'Really?' She's right, of course. So far, I've been winging it. 'Well, tell him to write them. It's a great opportunity.' What do we pay these guys for anyway?

The next few days are hell. A weasel-faced kid called Jan Hagelmann, a trainee on loan from Frankfurt, sits outside my office working on a laptop, poring over figures, producing draft after draft of numbers, graphs and charts. I can barely understand half of what he gives me, and several times fly into a rage, tearing up presentations and throwing them across the room at him.

What really pisses me off is that he never really reacts. The kids at Bartons used to tremble if a MD let rip at them – they could be fired in a heartbeat, and often were. But Jan has a German employment contract and he's bullet proof. The only thing I can do to him is make him work, and I go for it with a vengeance, making him stay late every night and work through the weekend, biking round revised drafts to me at home, which I return, unread, with comments like 'Hopeless' and 'No – start again. More detail!' or 'Bin this and do it properly – be more concise!' On Sunday night I call him in the office around ten o'clock.

'Still there, Jan?'

'Yes, Mister Hart.'

'And you haven't finished?'

'No, Mister Hart.'

'Really, Jan – you can't be very good, can you?'

By Monday night he's exhausted. I stop by his desk, confirm that he's e-mailed the latest version of the presentation to me and to Frankfurt, and tell him I think he's useless, unimaginative, bone-idle, and has no future in investment banking.

Christ, I love my job. Nowhere else in the civilised world could you treat another human being like this and get away with it.

♦ ♦ ♦   *Except for journalism*

It's Tuesday morning, and I'm flying to Frankfurt with Paul and Two Livers. He looks like a male model, tall, sleek, not a hair out of place. He's wearing a conservative, pale blue suit from Brooks Brothers, a white shirt and a dark blue tie

from Salvatore Ferragamo. Two Livers looks like Miss World with a brain – pale grey trouser suit from Armani, white collarless blouse that buttons up to the top, with a small gold crucifix around her neck and – get this – no earrings and very little make-up. She's sipping a bloody Mary, and looks earnest, studious, the kind of woman you'd definitely take seriously, and yet at the same time you'd want to rip her panties off. At least I would. In fact the other night I did, but that's another story.

Technically they are both still on 'gardening leave' from their old firms, but everyone knows that certain rules are there to be broken, and they've already been out hiring people, dealing with head-hunters, ordering new systems and infrastructure, and generally planning the move to a much larger new building in Docklands – our European flagship headquarters, which we've labelled the Pleasure Palace, and which will recycle the kind of money that even Frankfurt will notice. They're energised and excited.

By comparison I'm dull, grey and depressed. I feel like a condemned man. It's as if I've already been found out, and now I'm going to have to own up that I really shouldn't be these guys' boss, more like their bag carrier. They each have more talent and experience in their little finger than I have in my entire body. Gloom and depression start to set in, the black dogs are circling, and I can feel myself sliding into danger.

In the nick of time, like a life preserver that inflates automatically on hitting the water, my investment banker's self preservation instinct kicks in. I remind myself that it really doesn't matter who runs an investment bank, as long as they vaguely look the part. You could pick more or less anyone at random from most trading floors, tell them they're in charge, and for as long as they didn't blink, everything would be fine. Achievement doesn't so much come from effort by management, as the state of the markets, the amount of corporate activity, and whether your firm happens to be around at the right time. This is normal, so don't panic. I start to feel better.

We're sitting in Club Class, which means nothing on these short-haul European flights. Every seat is taken by businessmen, bankers, lawyers, accountants, management consultants, the faceless grey masses swarming all over the world's business centres. The overhead lockers are full, so my briefcase is shoved under the seat in front of me, the hot breakfast smells nauseating, and I know I'm going to get off the flight at the other end looking and feeling sweaty, crumpled and tired. I make a mental note that next on my shopping list has to be a smoker – a private jet like Rory's. If I survive.

In Frankfurt we're met at the airport, whisked into town in a Grossbank limo, and greeted at the bank by Herman and some of his team. They show us into a large auditorium, where after ten minutes or so a couple of hundred middle-aged Germans file in and sit down to stare at us as if we are some kind of exhibit. These are the regional managers, the men who manage the lifeblood of Grossbank, its access to all the hard-working, wealthy citizens who are paying my bonus. They look sceptical, unconvinced, as if they are here on sufferance.

I take my place on the podium, flanked by Paul and Two Livers. Herman has disappeared – apparently he's too senior in the German hierarchy to attend this sort of meeting, which makes me even more nervous. One of Herman's flunkies stands up and starts talking in German, which I don't understand, except for a reference to 'Doktor Hart'.

'Doktor Hart'? It's well known that Germans are a highly educated people, spending far longer than the rest of us at university, and have great reverence for titles – they apparently call it *Titelfreude*, the joy of titles. It says something about our two nations that in England we have the joy of sex, in Germany the joy of titles. I have no idea if Herman's flunky knows I don't have a doctorate, but I make a note for future reference. Over here, this stuff counts.

The flunky finishes, and indicates that I should step forward to the lectern. There's a clear plastic idiot board in front of me for me to read my presentation from – or Jan's presentation, since he wrote it – and a laptop to advance the

Powerpoint slides. I went through it all last night: lots of numbers, charts, graphs, organograms, enough to bore the most heavyweight investment banking anorak rigid.

'Gentlemen, good morning.' A few heads incline in my direction, but otherwise no reaction. I click on the laptop, and the introductory slide appears: 'Grossbank's future in investment banking'. I look at the idiot board and read off it. 'My name is Dave Hart.' Thanks, Jan – I probably could have managed that one myself. 'I'm an investment banker. I'm here today to tell you about Grossbank's exciting plans to go forward into the twenty-first century.' This is pretty banal, dumb stuff. I don't recall it from the previous versions. If you don't grab an audience like this in the first thirty seconds, you're toast. Click to slide two – 'One key message'. I read off the idiot board again. 'I have one key message for you today. If you take away nothing else from this presentation, remember this.' Click to slide three: 'You're on your own, pal.' I read off the idiot board: 'You're on your own, pal.'

Shit! I click on rapidly, but all the other pages are blank, and nothing's coming up on the idiot board. I glance across to Paul, but he shrugs his shoulders helplessly. That dumb, fucking kid Jan Hagelmann just committed career suicide. Doesn't he know I kill people? I'll wring his fucking neck. I look out at the audience. They are frowning, trying to work out where I'm coming from, what this is leading up to.

'We all are. Every one of us. We come into this world alone and we leave it alone. It's what we do along the way that defines us.' I pause and stare out into the middle distance, wondering what the hell to say next. 'That's why I'm not going to give you a formal presentation this morning.' I can't. I don't have one. 'I could tell you how we are going to unleash a tiger in the world's markets, how this firm's enormous financial resources are going to be put to work behind the best teams, the finest people in the industry, and how we are going to come from nowhere and sweep the board with our competition. I could bore you endlessly about the business streams we've already identified where this firm will be a top-three player within three years. I could show you projections for the obscene profits that will be thrown off by the great financial engine that we will create.' I need to change tack fast, because some of them are whispering to each other, probably wondering what I am going to tell them. Maybe if they have any ideas, they could share them with me. 'I could tell you all of that, and it's all true.' Yes, honestly. 'But it won't happen overnight. It will require patience and forbearance and enormous investment, and still it won't be easy. But life isn't meant to be easy. Life is about challenges, and you face those challenges best with friends and comrades alongside you.' I could add that there is no comradeship quite like that created by millions of pounds of guaranteed bonuses, but these people get paid peanuts, so I don't. 'So I'm going to talk to you instead about people. Our people. The real people inside these suits.' What the hell can I say next? That the 'real' us are driven by shallow, materialistic greed and alcohol and drug-fuelled lust? That we'd sell our soul for a bigger package, say 4 x 4?

I point to Two Livers. 'You will come to know my colleague, Doktor MacKay, over the coming years as someone who is constantly pressing you for introductions to corporate clients in your regions for potential investment banking business. You'll think her a dragon, a demon in woman's clothing, who is constantly demanding more.' Though not quite the way she was demanding more from me the other night. 'But on Sunday mornings you would see a very different Doktor MacKay. On Sunday mornings you'd find her on her knees…' Preferably kneeling at my feet, and you can guess what she'd be doing. '…Doktor MacKay is a lay preacher.' She can certainly get preachy after she gets laid, especially on the subject of senior management incentives.

I glance to my right. Bang on cue, Two Livers touches her crucifix, then looks down modestly at the desk in front of her and tilts her head to one side. She looks like an angel. I could kiss her… at least.

'Paul…' I gesture towards Paul, sitting behind me on the other side. '…Paul is gay.' I pause meaningfully for this news to be absorbed around the room. The great thing about Germans is that they are on the whole very liberal-minded – they have this huge tolerance thing, which has come to be an article of faith among the educated classes. 'Paul knows what it's like to be alone. He knows what it's like to suffer because you're different. During the week, Paul will be a demon of the markets, but at weekends he spends his time counselling young men.' Generally after he's shagged them. 'He doesn't talk about what he does at weekends.' You wouldn't, would you? 'But he's as driven by what he does out of hours as what he does during the working day.' A fucking sex maniac, from what I've heard.

I can feel a change in the room. This isn't what they expected. Weakness, vulnerability, concern for one's fellow man, coming from investment bankers? Nah, get out of here. But I can sense that I've got them.

'Some of you may have heard wildly exaggerated rumours, tittle-tattle really, about my alleged salary and bonus package. I'm not going to dignify those rumours with a comment.' Mainly because they fall well short of the truth. 'But let me assure you of one thing. Half of everything I actually do earn goes to good causes. Not ten per cent, as some religions require, certainly not the few per cent that many of you voluntarily pay in church taxes. Half goes to good causes.' Fucking good causes. Like women's causes in Eastern Europe and Latin America. In fact I'm spending so much of my after tax income on these good causes that even on my enormous package I'll soon have to slow down.

'Remember the words of that truly great philanthropist, Andrew Carnegie, that he who dies rich, dies disgraced. It's who we are that matters, and how we live our lives. That's what I wanted to talk to you about today.' I search for something really fatuous to wind up with. 'Gentlemen, we're not alone. We're all in this together with our values and our beliefs – one dream, one team, one firm.' I clench my fist and wave it in the air. 'Grossbank rocks! Thank you.'

Phew, now I can go and kill Hagelmann. I pause, waiting for some polite applause. But then the strangest thing happens. The guys in the audience start banging the tables in front of them. What is this, a riot? Are they going to start throwing things? I turn to Two Livers and Paul. 'Let's get out of here.'

We rush to the exit, trying to ignore the ever louder banging behind us, and Herman's flunky hurries after us. When we get outside, I turn on him, furious. 'Do you have their names?'

'Y – yes, of course.'

'Good. Fire everyone in the room.'

'Wh – why? They liked you. They loved you. That's why you got this response. I've never known it before.'

'You mean…' I do an impression of a fist banging a table.

'Yes.'

'Good. That's what I thought. So what I want you to do is fire everyone off a message from me, saying how much I enjoyed meeting them, but this is only the beginning. I want me and my team to spend much more time really getting to know all of them. Fire them all off something like that straight away.'

As Paul and Two Livers fall in behind me to take the lift to the fifty-fourth floor, both of them goose me. I grin. The A-Team.

◆ ◆ ◆

Doktor Biedermann looks like the villain Blofeld in the Bond movies. Bald, bespectacled rather than wearing a monocle, but with the same slow, deliberate movements. All he lacks is a cat sitting in his lap to stroke.

I'm sitting in his office with Herman, around a coffee table well away from his huge power desk. Paul and Two Livers have had to wait outside – some sort of German hierarchy thing. The wall to one side is what the Americans call a 'Me Wall'. I didn't know the Germans went in for this, but since I'm meant to

look at it, I do. There are photographs of Biedermann with the German Chancellor and President, and various dignitaries that I'm sure I should recognise, but don't. There's a set of shelves with various Lucite deal tombstones, family photos, and some interesting *objets* – highly appropriate fossils, which presumably he's collected himself, and some spectacular quartz crystals. I check out the family photos and do a double take when I see a shot of a family group and spot a familiar face. I turn to Biedermann.

'Isn't this…?'

'Yes. My nephew, Jan Hagelmann. I understand he helped you prepare your presentation today, which was so successful.'

Fuck. Jan the dead man. I was already fantasising about the torture I would put him through before setting him up for an exit that even a German employment contract couldn't stop. 'Yes. He's brilliant. Wasted in London, but brilliant, nonetheless.' It's bad enough having Maria reporting back to Frankfurt on me, without Biedermann's personal spy as well.

'Wasted in London? Surely not. I thought London was where the action is.' Biedermann looks across to Herman, who for once seems less sure of his ground.

'Doktor Biedermann, we need bright people everywhere, and most of all here in Germany, where our franchise is strongest. Someone with Jan's talent should be here, at the sharp end, showing by example what can be achieved.'

Herman looks briefly grateful. 'How would you use him here in Germany?'

'Leave that to me. I've had it in mind from the outset to put really bright, sharp young Germans into the field, somewhere relatively small, but where they can have a big impact.'

Biedermann and Herman are both nodding. 'Good. We'll follow this with interest.'

We are briefly interrupted by the arrival of two more fossils in the room. Both come in, shake hands, mutter their names, which I instantly forget – apparently they are members of the supervisory board, which sits above the management board, and is even more fossilised.

Biedermann leans back in his chair and forms a bridge with his hands, savouring the moment. 'So, Mister Hart.' It's that *Titelfreude* thing again. 'I know it's still early in your time at Grossbank, but some of us…' He looks at the two fossils, who nod their heads wisely, avoiding eye contact with Herman and me. '…some of us feel that it is important to take stock of the direction in which the London operation is heading. To us it seems that so far, all we have achieved is to fire our existing people – people of long service and great loyalty – spend vast sums hiring expensive people from other firms, announce grandiose schemes for a new building, which will cost us further millions, and we have yet to see a concrete business plan for the board to approve.' He leans forward, fixing first Herman, and then me, with a stare. 'Or am I wrong?'

There's clearly a power play going on here between the old guard and the new. The old guard probably liked the bank the way it was: rich, successful and secure. If it isn't broken, don't fix it. The new guard are bored, greedy, and envious of their British and American peers. They want a new train set. It's clear whose side I'm on.

When Herman doesn't respond, I take it as my cue.

'Gentlemen, the reason I haven't presented a detailed business plan is obvious.'

They all look at me, and even Herman seems puzzled.

'We don't have one.'

Herman looks horrified, and the others sit back smugly, an ugly grin spreading over Biedermann's twisted features.

'If we did have one, I'd have to ask you to fire me.'

'What?' Now they're really puzzled.

'If at this juncture, I was tying the bank's future to a specific, single plan, no matter how well devised, I'd be dumb and you'd have to fire me.'

Biedermann is nodding. He's looking forward to firing me. Didn't think it would happen quite this soon, but he's relishing the prospect.

'Gentlemen, there's a saying in English that goes back to the early dawn of warfare: no general's plan ever survived the first shot of battle. We could come up with a plan, sure we could. We could hire management consultants and have long navel-gazing sessions, playing games of fantasy investment banking until the cows come home. But we'd get nowhere. Analysis paralysis. Or we can be like the Special Forces. Parachute into the jungle with a crack team, an unbeatable team and win! Someone far older and wiser than me once said of strategy in investment banking that the only point in having one is so that at year-end you know what you've departed from. I can't tell you what markets are going to do, or rates, or what sort of corporate activity will occur over the next twelve months. We can guess, we can speculate, we can make predictions, but ultimately we have to create a team, a business, that is flexible, responsive, pragmatic. They say elephants don't sprint, but this elephant will dance and sprint!' I tap the table top with my finger. 'Gentlemen, our plan is not to have a plan! We'll assemble the best of the best, equip them with state of the art systems, put the weight of the bank's capital behind them, and then sound the bugles and charge.'

I make my voice drop to a whisper. 'And we will win. That will be the legacy of the investment banking initiative in years to come. In years to come, when people take it for granted that Grossbank is a major force in global investment banking. That, gentlemen, will be your legacy to future generations.'

Silence. Then, from Biedermann, who looks to be seething, a slow hand clap. The fossils glance at him, irritated. My little speech may actually have got their pulse going again briefly. He can see they are not with him. Herman pulls out a handkerchief and mops his brow. Dumb move, Herman. Don't ever play poker.

'Mister Hart. You make a very good case for not planning. But in this bank we are accustomed to doing things after we have thought them through, not before.

You have shown you can destroy what the bank built over many decades in the London office. You have shown you know how to spend money. But you have not won any new clients, Mister Hart. That is what I would like to see. Where are the clients? Gentlemen, I propose we meet again in one month's time to review progress. And I will be expecting news of clients.'

Herman's visibly relieved. He's off the hook, at least for now. The fossils nod their agreement, and a few minutes later I'm standing in the anteroom to Biedermann's office, where Two Livers and Paul are waiting.

'How did it go?'

'Great, we've got one month to make it work.'

They both smile. They know when I'm joking. I wink at Two Livers. 'Better have fun while we can.'

◆ ◆ ◆

Jan Hagelmann is finally crying.

He's standing in my office, in front of my desk, while I lounge in my chair, feet on the table, staring out of the window.

'Y – you really agreed this with my uncle?'

'Yes. And Doktor Schwartz. It'll be good for you. And good for the bank too. I'm told that Gruenkraut is very picturesque. It may be a quiet sort of place, with an ageing population, and not quite the night life of London, but it's only an hour-and-a-half from Munich.' I swing my chair around and give him an enthusiastic smile. 'And it's a challenge. If you can show the people at our branch offices that even the dullest, sleepiest, most boring village in Germany can produce the goods if it's tackled properly – why, the sky's the limit.'

'But… why three years?'

'Three years? Why because that's how long it takes to get to know a place, find your way around, identify the key people in the local business community, cultivate them, and eventually… bite them in the neck. The way investment bankers do. Now get out of here.'

I know I shouldn't enjoy this, but I do. The same way I enjoyed sitting at my computer and ordering nine-hundred dollars' worth of postgraduate degrees and diplomas from American universities first thing this morning. They'll be going up all over the back wall of the office. And Maria has the presentations team working their Adobe Photoshop image editing software to produce a whole new set of shots of me. They all think it's another one of my little eccentricities, or some practical joke.

How wrong they are.

Right now, I need to find clients. So I do what all investment bankers do when they need to justify their existence at team meetings or in front of their bosses: I read the paper. Some would call it ambulance chasing, because by the time a deal reaches the newspapers, the firms that are working on it have long since been appointed. If it's a piece of business requiring a group of banks to be formed – a syndicated loan, say, or a share sale or bond issue – then there might still be a chance to squeeze a few crumbs from someone else's table. For the price of a newspaper, you at least get the chance to say, 'Sadly this time we only had a co-management position in MegaCorp's issue, because our terms were a few basis points away from Hardman Stoney's, but next time we'll be more aggressive.' Never underestimate the importance of the press.

On the inside pages, there's a feature on the private security companies working in the Gulf. They're employing thousands of armed guards, mostly ex-military, to protect government employees and companies engaged in rebuilding Iraq. They've got people in Afghanistan too, on private contracts, doing close protection and armed escort work. The editorial slant of the article is that it's a bad business, with poorly organised, greedy companies sending ex-squaddies into harm's way without proper training or preparation. Hell, I bet some of them don't even have business plans.

The biggest firm out there, with multi-million dollar contracts, is called Military Overseas Security Solutions, or MOSS for short. They have nearly five thousand pairs of boots on the ground, huge contracts from the British and American governments, friendly Middle-Eastern regimes, and blue chip corporate names. They are the only firm in the region that the paper gives the thumbs up to, run properly and efficiently by a former trooper in the Special Air Service, called Mike Moss – hence the name.

These companies are private, because they probably think they could never float on the stock market. Too difficult a business, lots of legal problems, duty of care to their employees, nature of their work, too little transparency, I can see all the reasons why investment bankers would put them in the too difficult tray.

But we're not most bankers. We're Grossbank, and we're desperate.

The only thing against MOSS in the article is that some of their guys on the ground have put bumper stickers on their vehicles saying things like 'MOSS – no messing' and 'MOSS – peace through superior firepower.' It's the sort of thing that most banks' new business committees would get twitchy about. Luckily it doesn't bother my new business committee, because I'm it.

'Maria!'

I tell Maria to track down Mike Moss and get me a meeting.

One swallow doesn't make a spring. I need more firepower behind me if I'm to survive another month. I've got an idea – something Two Livers mentioned on the flight back from Frankfurt. She's arranging a meeting with the European Chief Investment Officer of Boston International Group, the London arm of one of the world's largest fund management firms. In the old days, he would never have given Dave Hart the time of day, but now, with Two Livers vouching for me, his door is open.

Irritatingly, in the midst of all this activity, I have to see Wendy. She's had my letter of employment for a few weeks now, and we need to resolve things between us. She doesn't want to stay out in Buckinghamshire, she wants to come back to Chelsea. And if we are going to split, then she agrees – or rather her lawyer does – that we should make it as amicable as possible – i.e., she'll take legal advice, but hopes that I won't. Based on my stated income of seventy-five thousand a year plus a season ticket loan, with uncertain bonus prospects, no savings, accumulating debts, and the need to finance Samantha through her education, they are proposing an out of court lump-sum settlement. She's sent me papers that are ready to sign. She wants a 'clean break', that would leave me free for the future - probably because her lawyer's told her that an MD picking up seventy-five thousand a year at a sayonara place like Grossbank is clearly going down the toilet. She knows it's an onerous sum for me to raise, and imagines that I would have to take on considerable borrowings, but perhaps Grossbank would advance me the money?

She wants two million pounds. I nearly laughed when I heard. The first rule of a City marriage has to be: tell your wife nothing.

We meet again in the coffee bar.

'Two million? How on earth can I raise that kind of money? Are you trying to kill me, or what?'

My face starts twitching, and she reaches out to touch it, a spontaneous, natural gesture of affection that twists an unexpected dagger of guilt in my gut.

I pull away. 'Don't. We're not close any more. It can never be the same and you know it.' Our eyes meet across the table, and I can see that hers are full of tears. 'I've moved on. It's only fair that you should know that there's someone else in my life now. It's hard work, but I'm making an effort.' And what an effort! There are actually dozens of people in my life now: Lithuanians, Estonians, Romanians, Ukrainians, Argentinians, Brazilians, Columbians; it feels like half the United Nations. What they have in common is that they are all under twenty-five, have great bodies and if the money's right, they are insatiable. And I love them all. Honestly. And then of course there's Two Livers, an exceptional perk for any man.

Wendy appears shocked and terribly upset. I don't know what she was thinking. Maybe two million would be an impossible sum for me to raise. For 'old' Dave Hart that would have been true. But 'new' Dave Hart could write her a cheque tomorrow. Or maybe it's the fact that she thinks I've found someone else dumb enough to take on a loser like me. Maybe it was me she was hoping for. Nah! I look at the document lying on the table between us.

'I don't know how I'm going to finance this.' I shake my head theatrically. 'But if this means we can draw a line and move on, and can still be friends, and do the best for Samantha, then I'll sign.' I slowly, reluctantly, get my Mont Blanc pen from my in-breast jacket pocket and carefully unscrew the top. I look up at Wendy, who still seems stunned by the turn of events. I can imagine the conversation with her lawyer – 'You're perfectly safe. It's win – win. There's no way he can sign this, but if he does, you should celebrate.' But they underestimated Dave Hart. As if forcing myself to be decisive, I sign the paper in a flourish, put the pen away, wipe my eyes with my handkerchief and leave without saying another word.

Outside, I hail a cab to the office, and glance back briefly to see Wendy sitting, shaking her head, crying her eyes out, mascara staining her cheeks as she stares at the papers I've just signed.

Christ, I'm good.

◆ ◆ ◆

Tim Turner is one of the most powerful fund managers in the City of London. Boston International Group – 'BIG by name, BIG by nature' – runs mutual funds, pension funds, unit and investment trusts, high net worth portfolios, hedge funds – you name it, they have it. They are a top three commission payer to every investment bank and broker in town. When they say 'jump', the investment banks ask 'How high?'

Turner himself is tall, very overweight, inclined to sweat profusely from even minor effort – like getting up from his desk to shake hands – and oozes arrogance from every pore. His jacket is slung over the back of his chair, his shirt sleeves are rolled up, his tie loosened, and he has bright red braces with black dollar signs and the initials BIG monogrammed on them.

His nickname in the markets is 'Tripod Turner', because apparently he's the biggest swinging dick of them all. In the cab on the way over I ask Two Livers if she wants to comment on that, but she smiles and stares enigmatically out the window.

We sit down in his huge corner office – even larger than mine – get the pleasantries over with and the coffee poured, and I start to explain why we've come.

'Mister Turner, you may have heard that Grossbank is intending to become a major force in global investment banking over the next few years.'

'Yeah, I heard the Germans have decided it's their turn to step up to the plate and pour money down the drain. Someone has to keep house prices rising in London.'

I smile, as if in appreciation of his little joke. Wanker!

'Grossbank doesn't yet have a presence in asset management outside Germany.'

'You don't have anything at all outside Germany – apart from yourself and Two Livers and Paul Ryan, plus a few hired guns I hear you're taking on.'

'What the market hasn't yet realised is how serious we are. We're following a two-pronged strategy: build, and buy.'

'Buy? What are you going to buy? Do you want to buy BIG?' He laughs, a sort of snorting noise that makes his vast bulk shake.

'That's why we're here.'

He laughs properly this time, a great thigh slapping roar. We sit patiently, not reacting. Eventually he subsides, and looks at us speculatively.

'Are you serious? BIG would be a stretch even for Grossbank. And you guys aren't exactly players.'

At this moment, with immaculate timing, Maria calls on his secretary's number. From the corner of my eye I see his secretary get up from her desk, approach the big glass-walled office, and knock discreetly before entering.

'I'm sorry, Tim, but Mister Hart's secretary is on the phone.' She turns to me. 'You have an urgent call from George Soros. She wants to put him through now.'

'Later.' I wave my hand dismissively. I look at Tripod Turner. 'Of course we're serious.'

For the first time, he looks flustered, as his secretary shrugs and returns, muttering, to her desk to explain to Maria that I can't take Mister Soros's call right now.

Turner points out to where his secretary is sitting. 'Was that *the* George Soros?'

'No.' I shake my head emphatically.

'No?' Now he's really confused. In fact it was Maria, my secretary, following the instructions I gave her before we left.

I turn to Two Livers. 'Go for it.'

She nods, crosses one beautifully tanned and streamlined leg over the other, and starts reading from her notes.

'Let's talk about BIG. You're currently capitalised at around eleven billion dollars, and closed last night in New York at eighty-five dollars a share. Employees own forty-three per cent of the company, and your own stake is close to seven per cent.'

He nods and says nothing. At least we have his attention.

'You also have employee options to buy shares at ninety dollars. Ten million options for yourself alone, and a lot more are held by your colleagues. These were issued a few years ago when the company was in trouble. There was a management crisis, and the board felt it had to lock in key personnel. But the shares have never traded that high – the market seems to know that ninety dollars could trigger the exercise of a raft of options and the release of a lot of shares into the market, and it acts as a kind of ceiling on the share price.'

Again he nods.

'These employee options are about to expire in six weeks' time – worthless, unless the stock goes through ninety bucks.'

'You don't need to rub my nose in it.'

I take over. 'We're not. We're going to make you a happy man, Mister Turner. Tomorrow morning, Grossbank is going to announce that it's going into the market to acquire a strategic stake in the company, and that we don't rule out eventually making a bid for the entire firm.'

'Are you crazy? Tomorrow? The whole firm?'

Funny how even the biggest swinging dicks are only human.

Two Livers takes over again. 'We're not really planning to go through with it. BIG really would be too much, even for Grossbank to swallow.' Funny how we both look at her when she says the word 'swallow'. She could add that our board in Frankfurt don't actually know about this yet, but that's detail, and I like to think I'm a big picture man. 'Tomorrow morning we'll acquire a small stake in your company, which we are sure will be a good long-term bet for our share-holders. We won't actually commit ourselves firmly to bidding for the entire company, but we'll say enough to make sure your stock goes through the roof. If it doesn't hit a hundred dollars by the New York close, I'll give up drinking.' She reaches down to her handbag and takes out a small bottle of Evian water. At least it says on the bottle that it's Evian water. She unscrews the top and takes a long drink while we both watch. Then she looks down at her notes and adds, as if as an afterthought, 'Oh, and your ten million ninety-dollar options, currently worthless, will look quite attractive again. If you exercised them at ninety dollars with the share price at a hundred, you could make ten dollars a share times ten million… that's a hundred million dollars.' She turns to me. 'Not bad for a day's work.'

I nod. 'Not bad.'

He jabs his finger at us. 'Why are you doing this? What's in it for you?'

Two Livers smiles. 'We're in the happiness business. We want to make you happy.'

'Bullshit.'

I take over again. 'Let me put it this way, Mister Turner. We're not going to lose money on this transaction. It's good business. And Grossbank doesn't have many friends in the City of London.'

'So what?'

'So we want to be your friend.'

♦ ♦ ♦

After another night of relentless drugs, booze and hookers, even my stamina's being tested. Today is a 3G day – I feel I'm labouring under three times the force of gravity. Worse yet, I'm actually starting to get bored. Really!

Did I say drugs? Okay, I am getting into drugs in a minor way, and probably have been for a little while now, but only coke, and not every night. It's far more common than you might think, and it's pretty harmless really. It gives me a buzz, keeps me flying. The girls bring it with them – it's a way for them to earn a little extra pocket money on top of what I give them.

The shadows round my eyes are getting darker now, and my face seems more lined – more distinguished – and there are more grey hairs. I suppose I'm growing into my role, looking the part more, getting more miles on the clock.

Speaking of which, I perk up as I remember that today I get to pick up my new toy, a silver grey Bentley Azure convertible. An awesome, throbbing power machine, rather like her owner. I take a cab to the garage, have a half-hour briefing on how she performs – shame they don't offer this with women - then cruise round to Two Livers' flat in Mayfair, to collect her and take her down to Sussex, to a disused airfield that serves as the UK headquarters of MOSS.

Mike Moss looks like a wiry prop forward. He has wavy dark hair, broad shoulders and exceptionally large hands. He speaks in an almost unnaturally soft voice, and is quiet and deferential in the way that you can only ever hope to be if you enjoy complete confidence in your ability to kill any human being on the planet.

His office is spartan, as I half expected, with posters of weapons on the walls and photographs of convoys crossing deserts. The coffee is instant, from a jar by a kettle in the corner, and he makes it himself. It's a remarkably low overhead operation, even though it's picked up contracts worth eighty-million dollars in the last twelve months alone.

He's googled me, and starts by congratulating me on what I did to the 'bad guys' in Jamaica. We have the sort of conversation that you can only have between men who have faced the ultimate challenge and won.

'How was it?'

'Tough.'

'Did you think about it much afterwards?'

'Sure.'

'You always do the first time. I shouldn't say this, but it gets easier.'

Lots of things left unsaid, and probably best so in my case.

He's also checked out Grossbank, and in the nicest possible way, doesn't know what we can do for him. Under normal circumstances, he'd be right, but he doesn't know how desperate we are. I let Two Livers do the talking.

'Mike, this company needs additional financial resources to expand.'

'No, we don't. We're a cash machine. Completely flexible. Bring people in as we need them. Keep the overheads low. Look at this place. Costs nothing.'

'But you could certainly use additional funds.'

'No. We'd waste it. Right now, we're really well organised, tightly run and efficient. We don't hire officers. We let the lads get on with it. And it works.'

'But you personally could use some extra cash. It's not as if you haven't earned it.'

'No, I couldn't. I've already put aside more than enough to look after the family. And besides, the beauty of this place is that if the contracts come to an end, I can lock the door and go off and do something else.'

'But you've created considerable value in the company. A stock market listing would allow you to unlock that value. It would reflect the full extent of your achievement.'

'Who cares? Like I said, I don't need to.'

Exasperated, Two Livers takes a swig of Evian and throws in the towel. 'Mike, has anyone ever told you about greed?'

He smiles and rubs his chin. We're obviously not from quite the same planet after all. My turn.

'Mike, have you ever wanted to make a real difference?'

He shrugs. 'Sure. We all do.'

'Have you ever seen something that really makes your blood boil?' Like a Hardman Stoney MD with a bigger apartment than you?

'Sure. When we're in country, in both Iraq and Afghanistan, there's a huge amount of poverty, deprivation, local people whose lives are going nowhere. We support local projects where we can, with funds or supplies.'

Gotcha! 'Exactly, Mike – and that's what this is all about. You support local projects where you can. Mike, you could list this company on the Stock Exchange, sell shares for tens of millions of pounds, and put the funds into a charitable foundation that could really make a difference on a grand scale. Tens of millions, Mike. Think about the effect that would have at the sharp end.' He says nothing, but I can see I've got him. 'Come on, Mike. How can you just shrug your shoulders and walk away from that?'

On the way back we put the top down. I light a large Cohiba, which I feel is in keeping with the image of the car. It's a surprisingly warm late February day, with the first hint of an early spring. Better yet, as we drive through Horsham a loser in a BMW Z3 pulls alongside me at the traffic lights, looking across at me and revving his engine. I wait for the amber light to appear, then put my foot down and smile as the silver grey beast hurls itself forward, leaving him behind. He catches up at the next lights, and the same thing happens again. At the third set of lights he winds his window down and leans across.

'I think you're a sad git.'

I look at him and smile, take a puff on my cigar and nod. 'You're probably right.' Then I put my foot down again and leave him in the dust. Fucking hairdresser!

We get back to the office at two o'clock London time, half-an-hour before the New York opening. Paul has briefed our dealers, and all eyes are on the screens. We're going on an elephant shoot today – Grossbank will be acquiring a stake in the Boston International Group.

There's a lot of tension in the dealing room. Grossbank has never done anything like this before. Neither have I, but everyone has to start somewhere. As soon as the stock opens, our announcement goes across the wire and we're in there buying. This being the New York Stock Exchange, the reaction is instantaneous, and BIG shares go haywire. We pick up some in the high eighties, but within minutes they are in the mid nineties, before racing through a hundred dollars a share and settling at a hundred and five. We've managed to spend about four hundred million dollars acquiring a stake at the lower levels, before backing off and keeping our remaining powder dry.

It takes a little while for Frankfurt to realise something is going on, but when they do, Maria comes rushing over.

'Mister Hart – I've got Doktor Schwartz and several members of the board on the line insisting they speak to you urgently.'

I wander back to my office, flop down on my chair and put my feet on the desk. 'What line are they on?'

'Line three.'

'Okay, tell them to start talking. I'll pick up in a minute.'

She stops and gives me a strange look.

I grin at her and wink. I flick the phone to speaker.

'Dave Hart here. Good afternoon, gentlemen.'

For once, they ignore the formalities.

'What is happening? What are you doing? Are you mad?'

I try to be patient, talking in a mild, matter of fact tone. 'If you're talking about BIG, which I assume you are, it's a normal investment banking transaction, well within our remit. Gentlemen, I'm surprised that you're surprised. If I bothered you with every little thing, we'd never get anything done.'

'Every little thing? You have just announced that we are buying an eleven billion dollar company.'

'Actually, it's worth a lot more than that, since we started buying their shares. But let's not split hairs. We are not buying the company.'

'So why did you release this press statement?'

'Gentlemen, if you read the press statement carefully, you'll see it says simply that we are acquiring a strategic stake, and may decide to move to a full acquisition in the future. Well guess what? We just decided not to. If the stock stabilises around these levels we'll unload our position in a few weeks' time. BIG was trading at a discount to other comparable quoted fund management groups, because of a perceived overhang in the market caused by a large block of employee share options priced at ninety dollars. The upside was capped. Well, we just blew that cap away. Now the stock's free to trade at a higher level, and we'll cash in our chips as soon as we can. We'll tell the market we couldn't get a big enough stake and so we're selling.'

A long pause at the other end, then: 'We still don't like it. Why didn't you tell us?'

'We sent a full presentation by e-mail last night, for the attention of all management board members, the head of Frankfurt PR, and the supervisory board.' It's true. I told Paul to prepare it, and make sure it ran to at least a hundred pages, including appendices. 'You were told everything.' Silence. These guys probably can't even open e-mail. They rely on their secretaries to do it for them, and anything that runs to more than a couple of pages can't be important.

'Gentlemen – imagine it's 1939, and the tanks are rolling. They're five kilometres into Poland and you decide you don't like it. What are you going to do? Call them back?'

The line goes dead.

♦ ♦ ♦

I am fast becoming a legend.

Tripod Turner thinks I'm a genius and wants to buy me dinner. Herman the German is looking at a hundred and fifty million dollar profit on our BIG stake – now trading around a hundred and twenty dollars a share, actually ahead of other comparable companies, and Biedermann is so desperate to pick a hole in what I'm doing, he's coming to London with Herman and the fossils to have our next review meeting.

Maria is starting to like me, despite herself, and has thrown herself into the creation of my 'Me Wall', getting my various doctorates and diplomas from American universities framed along with the doctored photos from the presentations team. Whereas once I joked about her leaving her broomstick outside the office on hover, now I find I'm warming to her.

Best of all, I'm going to have a meeting with my – sorry, our – possible new PR advisers, Ball Taittinger. Bill Foreman, our London office PR director, has got them in to pitch their services to me – sorry, us.

They say that perception is king in the Square Mile. Get the smoke and mirrors right, and the substance will fall into line. So today we're going to talk about… me!

The team from Ball Taittinger are everything you would expect from a top PR firm – a grey-haired, craggy-faced, seen it all, knows everyone, goes to all the best places senior partner, who is slick, seasoned, ultra-smooth, and could be a senior investment banker, except for the pale pink tie; a much younger, mid-ranking adviser, who looks like he spends his out of hours time partying even harder than I do, and actually it's quite a privilege that he's struggled in to attend this meeting; and not one but two lots of eye candy – blonde and brunette – who surprisingly seem to have brains, probably did most of the back-ground work for today's meeting, and get major speaking parts in the presentation, possibly because the number two on the team is too shagged out to talk.

The presentation is called 'The Hart Enigma'. The moment the slide goes up, they've got the business. They really don't need to say anything else. But the girls go on to say how Grossbank needs to be associated in the public mind with me, my courageous action in Jamaica, my tough-guy, firm management style, and my vision for the future. Out with the old Grossbank, in with Dave Hart, modern day hero.

I try to appear detached. 'Isn't there a danger in creating a cult of personality around one man?'

The senior partner – in my mind, I've nicknamed him the Silver Fox - takes this one. 'An investment bank is no different from any other business. It has to deploy its assets efficiently and dispassionately, to best effect, regardless of the individuals involved. This is not about you. It's about the bank, and what's in the bank's best interest. In the case of Grossbank, the principal asset here in London is you. I know it's difficult to discuss people in this hard-nosed way, but you're effectively a device to be deployed with the media. People look at you and they see someone who is young, handsome, hugely successful, decisive, highly intelligent and yet willing to risk it all to save a little boy. All of that will play brilliantly with the media. It already has. We can use it to build a huge campaign around you – and completely re-invent Grossbank's image in the process.'

This is better than sex. Well, almost. 'Go on.'

'People see you as someone who has it all, yet still takes huge risks – a physically courageous individual in an age of selfishness. You're a maverick, charismatic, a natural leader, someone the best and brightest in the City of London will look to for leadership. Someone they'll follow into the unknown, with an exciting new venture that will revolutionise world markets.'

This is awesome. I could sit here all day. 'I see. What else?'

He pauses for a second, takes a breath, and goes on, speaking more quickly now. 'You'll go where others fear to tread. You left the security of a well-established firm – Bartons, a top UK name – and went into the unknown, into virgin territory, to shape your own destiny. You're a pioneer, and you're not afraid. You don't have to be. You've faced real danger and won. A man like you isn't afraid of anything that can happen in the stock market, or in some boardroom. You're Dave Hart!' He's standing now, clenching his fist with passion.

'Excellent. I'm convinced. Let Bill know what your fees are and we'll get started straight away. Maybe some profile pieces in the weekend papers? Anyway, I'll leave the detail to you.'

◆ ◆ ◆

Our newly formed equity capital markets team are working on Grossbank's first UK flotation, of the security company Military Overseas Security Solutions. The press coverage has been mixed. There are suggestions in the left-wing press that the MOSS Foundation is a cynical ploy to legitimise a dirty business. In the financial press there are questions about Grossbank's ability to get the deal done. Will we be able to put together a syndicate of banks for a potentially controversial deal? If we don't, will institutional investors buy shares in a company that may not be followed by other firms' research analysts, or traded by other firms' market-makers? Grossbank may be spending money to hire heavy-hitters, but one firm can't do it all.

I decide to make some calls. First I call Mike Moss. I explain that we're making good progress, the deal is shaping up well, and we're at the stage where we need to bring in a syndicate of other banks.

'Mike, this is a controversial deal. People don't know if it'll work, and so they're keeping their heads down. It's the first deal of this type led by Grossbank, and the oppo aren't exactly queuing up to help a new competitor get established. If we have to do it alone, we will. You know that. But I want to try another route first. I need your help.'

'Anything I can do, Dave.'

'Do you know the US military attaché at their Embassy in London?'

'Of course. Bill Fraser. Former Green Beret. Some of the boys from the Regiment worked with him in Gulf War One.'

'Is he well-connected in Washington?'

'Are you kidding? He's got a direct line to the Joint Chiefs of Staff.'

I mentally tick one box. 'Another question. Of the top four or five corporate clients that you work for in the Gulf, who's most dependent on you to keep their operations going?'

'Has to be Anglo Petroleum. They're rebuilding the main pipeline south. We keep it from getting blown up.'

Bingo! I tell him what I want him to do, then I call Tripod Turner. I need some weight behind this deal, and he's just the man to help.

Maria comes in to run through my diary. Wendy called – do I want Samantha this weekend? No, but I get Maria to send some presents round. The property search agent wants to show me a house in Holland Park. We fix a time. Am I still intending to see my chiropractor about my back this afternoon? Yes, and I'll probably work from home afterwards. And finally, a lady phoned who claims she knew me in Jamaica – Sally Mills.

Sally Mills? Yes, I'll definitely see her. My jaded appetite is rekindled by the thought of finding a way into her perfectly clean, practical white cotton panties.

She's free tomorrow morning, and there's just time to squeeze her in before Herman and Biedermann and the fossils arrive.

Life is looking up. I might be tired most of the time, I might feel as if I'm racing just to keep up with myself, I might even wonder in odd moments if this is really happening to me, but I'm having fun! Every day is different, and I'm starting to enjoy myself.

I put my feet on my desk, light a cigar, and blow smoke rings at the freshly installed 'No Smoking' sign.

◆ ◆ ◆

Sally looks as great as ever, in an innocent, wholesome, well-scrubbed way. Spring is definitely in the air, and she's wearing a pretty floral dress with a white cardigan and practical, flat brown sandals. We meet in a coffee bar not far from my office.

Things start badly. I lean forward to give her a friendly peck on the cheek, but instead she holds out her hand for me to shake. On closer inspection, she looks tired.

I'm at my solicitous best. If only I behaved like this all the time, and actually meant it, I'd be a really nice person. I ask after her, after Toby, whether he had any after-effects from that awful experience, and how about Jasper and Monty, and of course Trevor the teacher. I'm half hoping that she's going to break down at this point, cry on my shoulder, and say they're finished and she doesn't know what to do any more, and can I please hold her tightly and tell her everything's going to be okay? That way I'd definitely get into her panties.

But instead, she says how Trevor has shown her occasional press articles about me from the finance pages. How Grossbank seems huge and very powerful, and so much seems to have happened in my life in a very short time and I must be very important now, and she feels guilty for not having kept more closely in touch.

She asks about Samantha, and I explain that no, sadly it's as I feared, and I haven't had the chance to spend time with her. I could explain that I have a photograph of Samantha on my desk, and another in the apartment, and a small one in my wallet, so I don't actually need to see her. But I don't think Sally would like that.

The conversation goes on, and it gets more apparent that she's skirting round whatever the real issue is. My investment banker's bullshit-ometer is on overload. Time is short, and I cut to the chase.

'What's really on your mind, Sally?'

She takes a breath, obviously summoning up courage, and plunges in. 'It's Harry.'

'Harry?' Who the hell is Harry? Does she have a lover? Has someone got there before me?

'My brother Harry. He's Chief Executive of Hastings BioScience.'

My news filter generally blocks out items that aren't in some way relevant to my own well-being, so I have to dredge quite deep to remember.

Ouch. I can see why she's worried. HBS provide animal testing services for pharmaceutical and healthcare companies. It's a vital service to test new drugs that will one day save people like me from an early grave. HBS are interesting because they set out to do controversial work in an ethical, transparent way. They don't get involved in animal testing for cosmetics companies, and they limit their experiments to dread diseases and other dire medical conditions that contribute to the sum of human misery. So naturally the eco-terrorists are after them.

'Is he the one who was attacked? By the Animal Freedom Front? Didn't they beat him with baseball bats or something?'

She nods and gets a tissue out to wipe her eyes.

'Here – take this.' I hand her a new silk handkerchief from Harrods men's department. She wipes her eyes and goes to pass it back to me.

'No. Hang on to it. You can let me have it back next time.' Yes – next time! Hart, you're a pro. But she's still upset, so I tilt my head to one side, empathising with her as she summons up the courage to talk about this painful subject.

'They beat him about the head. He could have been killed.'

'Cowardly bastards.'

'He's very brave. He won't give up. I told him about you. He said he wishes he could be as brave as you.'

I look down at the table modestly. 'I did what anyone would have done.'

'But anyone didn't do it. You did. That's why I'm here today.'

Christ. I get a sudden nervous twinge. I hope she doesn't expect me to be brave twice in the same lifetime.

'Harry's firm are close to bankruptcy. Their building's like a prison camp, with barbed wire and police and security guards. Anyone going in and out is heckled by a mob of demonstrators. It's been going on for over a year now. The staff have to be escorted in and out of the premises, and even then they get followed home. They've been sent horrible things through the post – human excrement, hate mail – and now the bastards are targeting their shareholders and bankers. Anyone who owns shares in HBS has their name and address put up on a website, and has to live in fear of being attacked by these nutcases. Their bank has given notice that it can't carry on lending them money. Apparently they're in fear of what might happen to their own employees if they carry on – they say they have a 'duty of care' to their own people, which means Harry and his company just get ditched.'

'Awful.' I shake my head. 'Poor Harry must be at his wits' end.'

'He is. That's why I said I'd come to you.'

'Me? What can I do?'

'You can step in and finance them. Not you personally, but Grossbank.'

Is she mad? I can't really tell her that ever since Jamaica the mere sight of a black man with dreadlocks makes me nearly wet myself. Now she wants me to

take on the eco-nutters as well. No woman, no matter how wholesome she might be, no matter how great the challenge of the chase, can really be worth dying for.

'Sally, I hate to say this, but I can't help.'

'Why? It's so… so important. HBS will go bust in a matter of weeks if no-one helps. They're on the brink already. And if they go under, lots of important medical research will go with them. People will suffer, Dave, real people, who deserve not to be bullied by thugs.'

'I know… and if it were my decision alone, you know I'd be with you in a heartbeat. But I have to carry my colleagues along with me. If Grossbank were to step in now, we'd be putting ourselves into exactly the position that HBS's existing bankers are in. We have a duty of care to our people too. We're not paid to take risks.'

'Yes, you are.' Her reply is abrupt, her manner almost contemptuous. 'You're all paid millions. If anyone's not paid to take risks, it's the policemen who stand guard around the HBS building, who get in the way when the bricks are being thrown. Or the soldiers you see on the television. Soldiers don't get a fraction of what you earn, and look at the risks they take, or firemen, or lifeboat men…'

'Sally, please. Don't go on.' It's too fucking painful. 'You're right.' Her eyes suddenly brighten. 'I'll see what I can do. I have to warn you that it's very unlikely we'll be able to do anything at all, but I'll try. I'll give it my best shot.'

'Oh, thank you, thank you.' She throws her arms around my neck and gives me a wonderful, fresh, moist kiss on my cheek. It's a beautiful moment, and so of course I have to blow it. I glance at my watch, and it's two minutes before I'm due to be meeting Biedermann and the Inquisition. Damn, there's no time to mess around. And so instead of putting my hands gently on her shoulders, staring into her eyes and saying, 'Sally, I'd do anything for you, because the truth is that I've loved you since the day I first saw you', there's a terrible grinding of gears in my head and I find myself reverting to my nocturnal default mode and saying, 'I want you, Sally Mills. I want you in my bed tonight'.

Even as I say the words, I know I've blown it.

She recoils, blushes to her ears, picks up her handbag and virtually sprints out of the coffee bar.

I look at my watch. I'm due right now with Herman and Biedermann. Fool, Hart, fool. I peel off a tenner, drop it on the table and scoot.

◆ ◆ ◆

When I get back to the office, I find Biedermann looking at my 'Me Wall', studying it with intense curiosity.

'Gentlemen, my apologies – an urgent new business development meeting.' I shake hands with everyone and take a seat at the small conference table with Herman and the fossils.

Biedermann carries on looking at the exhibits lovingly hung by Maria and the presentations team.

'Did you really go to all these universities?' He looks at the various certificates and diplomas. 'Six different universities, all in America? Three doctorates?'

I'm not sure quite how to play this one, so I grunt something incomprehensible and busy myself with serving coffee. Herman seems amused.

'And is this really you?' Biedermann is staring at a photograph of me sitting between Putin and Bush at a dinner. It's next to one of me kneeling in front of The Queen at Buckingham Palace, obviously receiving some form of award, and another of me with Charles and Camilla at the reception that followed their wedding. His eyes follow the line of photographs along the wall: me shaking hands with Nelson Mandela; me on a podium with Bill Gates, addressing an audience; me playing golf with Tiger Woods. At least the face is me, and the girls have done a great job.

'You've obviously had a very full and varied life.' Germans aren't necessarily great on irony, so I'm still not sure how to respond to Biedermann, and instead I clear my throat and pull out a chair. Lucky for me I rejected the girls' less plausible efforts: me planting a Union flag at the top of Everest; me collecting a gold medal at the Olympics; me in a codpiece and tights holding aloft the prima ballerina of the Royal Ballet. I sent one of me singing on stage with Madonna to Samantha, wondering what Wendy would make of it.

'Doktor Biedermann – please take a seat. If you gentlemen are ready, I'll give you an update on where we are.'

'Before we do that…' Biedermann is giving me one of those *For you, Tommy, the war is over* stares. '…could we talk about my nephew Jan… in Gruenkraut?'

Herman is hiding his face in a handkerchief, and even the fossils are looking for something to stop them laughing. They probably haven't had this much fun since they were alive.

'Gruenkraut?'

'Gruenkraut. When you said you were thinking of sending him 'into the field', I didn't think you literally meant a field!'

'Well, Gruenkraut is a very beautiful place, quiet, but full of challenges and opportunities. Or so I'm told. And a good man will always create opportunities, wherever he goes.' Biedermann is seething, and his cheek is twitching. Perhaps it's infectious. Perhaps everyone who gets to work with me ends up with their cheek twitching. I decide to twist the knife. 'And besides, it's only for three years.'

Herman dissolves into a muffled sneeze, and Biedermann stares at him, not bothering to hide the full extent of his loathing for the younger man.

Maria enters and hands out some papers that Paul Ryan has prepared.

'Shall we go on to the business report?' By way of response, Biedermann turns and stares at the picture of me with The Queen. I ignore him and plough on. 'Gentlemen, these show our summary operating results. You'll see that the first quarter of this year significantly exceeds our entire contribution for the whole of last year.'

'That's because of your little adventure in America, with Boston International Group.' Biedermann has stopped even a pretence at civility.

'It's true that we have made more money on that one trade than on everything else the London operation has been doing, but most of the rest is what I call legacy business. It's what we inherited from... your time, Doktor Biedermann.'

'What do you mean, "from my time"? This is still my time. I am still a board member of this bank, or had you forgotten?'

'Quite right, Doktor Biedermann. Forgive me – a slip of the tongue.'

Herman is studying the figures. 'But even the old businesses are doing better now. Why is that?'

'Fear and greed. You spill a bit of blood, you dangle a carrot.' I look again at Biedermann. 'Never happened in the old days.'

I can see the old man is seething. The fossils seem content, and Herman obviously has his tail up. Biedermann tries one last gambit. 'What about clients? I said last time that I wanted to see progress with clients.'

'Our first corporate client transaction is underway as we speak. We are starting to market shares in Military Overseas Security Solutions, a UK-based security company, which is our first London Stock Exchange flotation.'

'And how is the transaction going? Have you formed a syndicate of banks underneath Grossbank to help distribute the shares? Are other brokerage firms going to follow the shares with their research analysts? Are they going to commit their capital to trade the shares?'

Bastard. He's just that little bit too on the nail with his questions.

'Why don't we hear from Paul Ryan, our Head of Markets?'

Biedermann has a twinkle in his eye. He thinks I've suggested Paul talks us through the deal so I can distance myself from it and set someone else up as the fall guy. As if.

Paul is summoned and introduced.

'Paul – Doktor Biedermann is concerned about our ability to form a syndicate of banks for the MOSS deal. Could you update us on where things stand?'

'Sure. I don't mind admitting we've been struggling.' Biedermann smiles smugly and nods an 'I told you so' to the fossils as Paul continues. 'It's been one of the hardest deals I've ever worked on.' Now Biedermann's grinning broadly. 'No-one wanted to know. It's seen as a controversial deal, tough to sell, tough to syndicate.'

'Exactly. I knew this would happen.' Biedermann can't contain himself. Herman is fidgeting uncomfortably and the fossils are staring ahead inscrutably. 'We should never have accepted this business. I knew it would fail. Gentlemen, Grossbank's investment banking efforts have failed before they even began!'

Paul smiles deferentially at Biedermann. 'Well, that's not strictly true, Doktor Biedermann. You see, this morning, there seems to have been a change of sentiment in the market.'

'Oh? What are you saying?'

'Bartons called our syndicate desk and asked to be allowed into the deal. Said they'd like to support it, and that they'd like to welcome us as a newcomer to the UK market.'

'Bartons? Why?'

Because the Chairman of Anglo Petroleum, MOSS's biggest client, called Sir Oliver Barton and told him to, you idiot. And Sir Oliver wants Bartons to lead the project financing for their pipeline. I intervene. 'Paul's probably too modest to say this himself, but he does have a certain reputation in the market. Pulling power.'

Paul smiles modestly. 'And Hardman Stoney, Berkmann Schliebowitz and Schleppenheim have all called up as well. They're all looking for a piece of the action.'

'Really? All of them want a place in our deal?'

Sure, arsehole! Because the Chairman of Hardman Stoney in New York wants to be the next US Secretary of Defence, the American head of Schleppenheim's UK operation sees himself as a future US Ambassador to the Court of St James, and Berkmann Schliebowitz were told by Tripod Turner that he'd send them on a three-month commission holiday if they didn't fall into line.

'Will all of them commit to research and market-making?'

'Already have. And so have a number of other firms who are not in the syndicate. Boston International Group gave us a lead order for ten per cent of the deal first thing this morning. They're making it a core holding in their flagship Omega Fund, and have put the word around that anyone dealing with the Omega Fund has to cover MOSS, the way they do all the core holdings.'

'So this will be a great success?'

Paul looks at me and we both shrug. 'Should be. You don't often get a following like that for a first-time deal by a new player.'

Biedermann gets to his feet and paces to the end of the office. He's staring at the photo of me with Nelson Mandela.

'The difficulty I have with this deal, gentlemen, is that it is a deal without soul.' He waves his hand dismissively. 'Soldiers for hire – call them whatever you like, but they are mercenaries.' He looks at Paul and me. 'Hired guns. Grossbank made its name and reputation historically as a bank that was grounded in principles. We stood for what was right, even if it hurt our profits. Many powerful German companies have experienced difficulties over the years. But we stood by them. Other banks – investment banks – would have disappeared. Not Grossbank.

'And because we stayed with our clients, because we stuck to our principles, we prospered.' He positions himself strategically standing behind the fossils and points at Paul and me. 'Where are your principles, gentlemen?'

Fuck it. It's him or me. This place isn't big enough for both of us. 'Doktor Biedermann, if you want principles, I'll give you principles. Not abstract concepts,

but real, down-to-earth, here and now principles. Grossbank is going to do something no other firm in the City of London is prepared to do.'

I certainly have their attention. Even Paul is wondering what I'm on.

'We are going to refinance Hastings BioScience.'

Beside me, Paul takes a sharp breath. The Germans seem nonplussed. They haven't heard of Hastings BioScience. Why would they?

'HBS is a British company that assists pharmaceutical and healthcare companies from all over the world to test pioneering medical advances for dread diseases – cancer, Parkinson's, Alzheimer's, HIV-AIDS, you name it. All of us may one day have reason to be grateful for their work. They're world leaders in what they do, and I believe we should support them.'

The Germans are nodding. Herman speaks first. 'In principle I don't see any reason not to.'

'That's the thing – it's a high risk business. Right now, they're on the brink of going bust. They're struggling with huge uncertainty over the future, workforce issues, corporate clients who can take their business overseas, the kind of thing that could make some management teams throw in the towel. But these people are different. They have a vision, a mission and a great future, if only someone will stand by them. I want that firm to be Grossbank – in the finest traditions of the firm.'

Biedermann is puzzled. 'In principle, subject to confirmation of the numbers and the appropriate credit checks being carried out, I cannot argue with you. Do you know the company well?'

'The Chief Executive is waiting for my call. With your agreement, gentlemen?'

They look at each other, shrug their shoulders and nod. Paul rolls his eyes towards the ceiling and gives me one of those 'What the fuck are you doing now?' looks.

I slap him on the shoulder and wink. 'Come on, Paul – nobody wants to live forever.' Except me. I want to live forever so that I can carry on shagging.

♦ ♦ ♦

The offices of HBS are rather like I imagine Fort Knox to be. Barbed wire fences, windows with metal shutters, and security cameras everywhere. Two Livers and I arrive in the Bentley, which is now bearing my new personalised number-plate: H1 PAY. I chuckle at what Wendy will make of it when she hears.

A crowd of low-lifers are hanging around outside the gates. Kids in dirty combat jackets and new age beads and earrings, with beards and funny hairstyles, holding placards and chanting and maintaining an uneasy truce with a row of policemen in bright yellow jackets. The drill at the gates is obviously well rehearsed. As we swing into the entrance, whoever is monitoring the security cameras presses a button so that the gates swing open and we can glide in past the crowd. The shouting picks up as they realise we are visiting HBS, and I slow down and open the window of the Azure.

'Why don't you all go home, have a shower and see if you can get a job?'

I put my foot down and swing inside to safety as the gates close behind us and the crowd surges forward to battle with the policemen.

Harry Peters looks remarkably like his sister, except that he definitely isn't shaggable. He's late thirties – probably around my age – and has the frazzled look of a man who's been pushed to the limit. Dark shadows around the eyes, the first grey hairs, shoulders that default into a slumped position, and lines on his face that have nothing to do with laughter.

I wonder briefly if he spends all his nights shagging hookers and doing whisky and drugs, but he's not an investment banker or a hedge fund manager, so how could he afford it?

He greets us in the lobby and looks past us to the crowd outside, where a full scale battle is underway. As we watch, two more vanloads of police arrive.

'I don't know what's got into them. They aren't usually that bad. Perhaps it was the car – they probably see you as capitalists or something.'

'Something like that,' agrees Two Livers, giving me the sort of dirty look that doesn't turn me on.

He shows us into his office and goes into an excruciating hero worship speech about everything Sally's told him. How his nephew doesn't seem to have had any after-effects from Jamaica, and even mentions how they are testing a new synthetic skin for burn victims that might be useful if I ever considered surgery for the scar on my forehead.

Is he kidding? This scar and I are old buddies now. This scar's my meal ticket.

Eventually he dries up, and looks rather helplessly at us. He reaches over to a photograph of a smiling red-haired woman – probably seven out of ten, certainly shaggable. She's holding a baby. I guess she's his wife. 'We're calling in the receivers in two weeks' time.'

There's a long, poignant silence. I can hear the crowd shouting outside, more police sirens, and in the office, a clock on the wall ticking. I turn to Two Livers.

'Your call.'

Two Livers has spent the whole journey down here telling me I'm wrong on this one. I need to think again, I really am going too far, we're not paid to do stuff like this, and why the hell have I involved her?

But now she turns to Harry and sighs.

'Two weeks?'

'We've got no choice. The board decided we have no alternative. Those people…' He nods towards the sound of the crowd. 'They've won. We're throwing in the towel.'

She shakes her head. 'No, you're not. The cavalry's arrived.'

♦ ♦ ♦

The journey back from HBS is mixed. We get out of the gates under a flurry of stones, bottles, eggs and rotten fruit. There's a major riot underway, more protesters are arriving and being matched with huge numbers of police. TV crews are recording what has clearly become a major incident. A police car is lying on its side, its windows smashed. As we speed away a Molotov cocktail flies through the air and explodes in the road behind us. We pass rows of police vans unloading officers in riot gear.

'Fucking parasites. Who do they think they are?'

Two Livers is sulking, swigging from a bottle of Evian. 'Why did you make it my call?'

'Because when you start getting hate mail at home, or parcels of human excrement through the letter box, or your name gets registered on paedophile websites, I don't want you to ask me for more money. It was your call.'

'But you're the hero. I don't want to be a hero. Just rich.'

We lapse into an uneasy silence, until the mobile goes and it's Paul Ryan.

'We just priced the MOSS deal. Top of the range and it's trading at a premium. Mike Moss says you're a hero.'

Two Livers looks at me. 'See what I mean?'

It gets worse. Some selfish bastard has had an accident up ahead and the traffic comes to a standstill. We're hemmed in by VW Golf's and white vans and everyone seems to have their windows open and the radio thumping out Thick FM. The sooner we get road pricing and the chance to clear these people off the road, the better.

When we get back to the office I call a team meeting to prepare for the next steps with HBS. They can't quite believe we're doing this. Neither can I. Everyone seems to be taking comfort from the fact that I'm so certain about what we're doing. If this is leadership, it's damned scary.

The whole thing needs to be perfectly stage-managed, so Bill gets in the PR team from Ball Taittinger.

In the middle of all this, Wendy calls, angry and suspicious. She was watching the television news about the riots at Hastings BioScience and saw footage of me leaving the premises in a Bentley with the number plate H1 PAY and a blonde beside me. What's going on? Before I have a chance to lie to her, she says she's already spoken to her solicitor, and she wants the flat as well.

Can you believe this? The bitch, the greedy cow wants to take away my home, my refuge, my beloved shag-pad. I tell her to fuck off and hang up, making a note to send Samantha some more presents.

Then I get another call. It's Sally Mills. She's crying on the phone. Harry's called her and told her what we're going to do. What I'm going to do. She's so grateful. I seize the moment.

'Sally – what I said last time, it was unforgivable. I want to apologise. I have to apologise. When can I see you again so I can put things right?' She hesitates at the other end. She doesn't want to piss me off, because Grossbank haven't actu-ally done anything yet. On the other hand, the prospect of us getting anything straight between us – as it were – may not be exactly what she has in mind.

'Dave, I'd love to, but…'

'No buts, Sally. I need to talk to you. The next few days will be hard. I'm put-ting everything on the line to do what's right. When are you free? Tell me, and I'll be there.'

How can you refuse a hero? We fix a date and she hangs up. There's still time for her to change her mind, but after tomorrow? Nah. After tomorrow she'll be gagging for it.

◆ ◆ ◆

The Silver Fox and his team from Ball Taittinger have done a fabulous job. The main conference room at Grossbank's London office is standing room only. Wall to wall media - not just the dailies and the broadsheets, but TV and radio, and of course the financial press, and the women's magazines too. They're here for me. Don't you just love it when a plan comes together?

I mount the podium with Harry Peters, and Two Livers and Paul Ryan sit on either side of us.

The Silver Fox has prepped some of the media already. There's a buzz that even I find quite intoxicating. And I know all about intoxication.

The press conference has been scheduled for twelve noon, in time for the lunchtime news bulletins, after the morning's news and announcements have been absorbed, and in plenty of time for tomorrow's papers.

'Ladies and gentlemen, thank you for coming here this morning. Some of you know me already, but for those of you who don't, I'm Dave Hart, global head of investment banking at Grossbank. Seated on my left is a man who has sadly become familiar to all of you over the last two years, Harry Peters, the Chief Executive of Hastings BioScience.' I go on to explain how Harry and the people at HBS have been threatened, physically assaulted, persecuted and slandered, and all by extremists of the worst kind, who refuse to work inside democratic processes, but ride roughshod over the rest of us in their single-minded quest to impose their will on the majority. I pay tribute to his stamina, his determination, and his courage, and I underline the vital contribution to medical research of controlled, properly managed animal testing. Yes, it's a horrible practice, but dread diseases are even worse. If we have to choose, then until there's some better alternative, it's clear where Grossbank stands.

There's a round of applause as he stands to speak.

'Ladies and gentlemen, I wasn't expecting to be standing here today.' He pauses, and it's not an act. The emotion is almost too much for him. He reaches down to the desk and takes a swig from Two Livers Evian bottle. His eyes light up and he's back again.

'I was expecting to be announcing the calling in of the receivers. It was almost over for HBS, and with us would have gone dozens of vital medical research programmes, hundreds of research jobs, and a good chunk of the future for the British pharmaceutical industry.

'The reason? Finance. No-one was prepared to stand by us. No bank, no finance house, no institutional investor would support us. Not because they disagreed with what we were doing. But because they were afraid. Well, one bank wasn't afraid. Grossbank has agreed to refinance all of our debt, giving us a fresh chance for the future, and granting a reprieve to all of the vital medical research that would otherwise have ceased. It took guts to stand up and be counted, and it won't surprise you that the man who did so was Dave Hart!'

A round of applause goes up. It's pretty unusual for journalists anywhere to applaud anything, and I get the feeling that half of them are thinking I've lost my marbles, but what do they know?

I lost my marbles long ago.

'Thank you, Harry. Ladies and gentlemen, you've been given copies of the press releases from both Grossbank and HBS outlining the transaction. If there are any questions we'll be glad to answer them.'

A reporter in the front row sticks his hand up. 'Eddie Strange, *Daily Post*. Mister Hart – you've got a reputation as a hard man, but aren't you concerned for your own safety and that of your staff in taking on the Animal Freedom Front?'

My staff? Nah – they're expendable. 'Naturally. But this decision comes from the highest level within Grossbank. I'm the man on the spot, and I'll do what I have to do. As a firm we'll take whatever steps are necessary to protect our people. We already have enhanced security in place, and this will be increased following today's announcement.'

'Mister Hart – I'd assumed you were the man behind this financing. Are you saying the decision came from higher up?'

'I'm proud the bank is taking the stand it is, but the real credit should go to this man…' I turn and point to the screen, and right on cue, an enormous photograph of Biedermann appears. 'Doktor Biedermann personally instructed us on this transaction. He's the man who should get the credit at Grossbank. He's a board member of long standing. You'll find his photograph and bio in your packs.'

'Dick Harper, *Wall Street News*. Why is Grossbank, a German bank, taking a stand like this for a British company? Is it your fight?' Awesome. I make a mental note to double the Silver Fox's fees.

'Thank you, Dick. This is everyone's fight. All of us are affected by this, whether we choose to walk by on the other side of the road or not. We've made this our fight, and we hope that others will join us. We're a new boy in town, but it doesn't mean we can't stand up and be counted.'

'Ralph Clark, *Evening Echo*. Isn't this just a cynical ploy by Grossbank to squeeze huge fees out of a company that's on the ropes?'

'Thank you, Ralph. I'm grateful that you asked that question.' And even more grateful to the Silver Fox for planting it. 'I have here a summary of Grossbank's earnings in this transaction.' A slide appears behind me, headed 'HBS re-financing: summary of earnings'. It's blank. 'And for those from the financial press, who want more detail, here's how that breaks down.' Another slide appears: 'HBS re-financing: detailed earnings analysis.' It's also blank. Some of the journos start tittering.

'Er… Dave, those slides you just showed us were blank.' More giggling. A few of them are looking at the Silver Fox, to see if he's embarrassed. They love it when a dog and pony show goes wrong.

'I know.' I look around the room, savouring the moment. 'We're waiving our fees on this transaction, and we're not charging any loan interest either. We're doing this one for love.'

◆ ◆ ◆

Later, when it's all over, and I'm sitting in my office, Mike Moss calls to congratulate me. 'Dave, I always knew you were different. I've met a few bankers in my time, but never anyone like you.' Luckily, I feel I know him well enough to be sure he's not taking the piss. Everyone else is. Everyone else thinks I'm mad.

'But Dave – watch your back. I worry for you. These Animal Freedom Front people are nutters, and even you need to sleep sometime.'

If he only knew. This weekend I went for thirty-six hours without sleep with Clarisse, a black girl from the Congo, and Breathless Beth, a twenty-one year old blonde from Texas. I'm starting to think I'm super-human, though I notice that Maria looks concerned whenever I come back refreshed from a visit to the gents'.

The Grossbank refinancing of HBS is lead item in the day's television and radio news, the switchboard have already received threatening phone calls from the AFF, and a few low-life's have gathered at the entrance to the Grossbank building, where police and private security guards are watching them.

On the other hand, we've had a dozen incoming calls from chairmen and chief executives of large companies wanting to meet us. Two Livers is following them up – all the principled individuals who would 'love to do something', but don't. Giving business to Grossbank could just become the next corporate fad.

Maria calls through to me. 'I have Doktor Biedermann's office on the phone.'

'Put him through.'

He's apoplectic, and I'm glad we don't have video-phones, so he can't see me fighting to control myself. No-one had ever heard of HBS in Germany, but now there's an angry crowd outside the Grossbank Tower, he's had threatening phone calls, the Greens are calling for an inquiry, and already posters are being put up around town by anarchists showing a caricature of him dissecting a kitten. The bank's security department have decided that he's going to be chauffeured around in an armoured limousine with a couple of bodyguards, and his wife has been advised to leave town. As if this wasn't enough, the media are all over him, and he's got to give a press conference in half-an-hour. What the hell do I suggest he says?

'Stick to your guns! Tell it to them the way you told it to me, here in London. You inspired me, so inspire them. It's all about principles, Doktor Biedermann, that's why we've done this.' It takes me a few seconds to realise he's hung up.

Maria brings me a sandwich at my desk.

'How's Two Livers doing?'

'Miss MacKay left a message to say 'five out of seven so far' – she said you'd know what it meant.'

Damned right I do. We're aiming to get the chairmen, chief executives, or finance directors of the largest UK-based pharmaceutical companies in here tomorrow, for an urgent meeting. It's payback time.

Right now, it's time for my osteopath. I tell Maria I'll be working from home after my treatment.

◆ ◆ ◆

Last night I had my first threatening phone call. The phone rang, around three a.m., just after the girls had left. Like a fool, I picked it up, and a scratchy, hate-filled voice, said 'We know where you live. Best look over your shoulder, Hart.'

I'd had most of a bottle of Scotch, a couple of amazing tablets that the girls brought, and I thought it was a joke.

'Dan Harriman, you wanker. Come on over, it's only three o'clock. I've just sent the girls away, but I can call and get them back.'

Silence at the other end, then the scratchy voice again: 'Dave Hart, we know where you live.'

'Stop being a wanker. How many hookers do you want? Have you got any drugs?'

Click. 'Brrr…'

I put down the phone.

'Wanker!'

When I get to the office, the day's papers are laid out on my desk. It was a quiet news day, and we've made a splash. The *Post* once again has the best headline: *Bankers with Balls take on AFF*. They have pictures of Biedermann and me. 'City hard man Dave Hart yesterday sent a message to the Animal Freedom Front: up yours!' The cartoon in *The Times* shows Biedermann and me on top of a tank with black crosses on it. A group of City suits in pin-stripes and bowlers on one side are cowering from a bunch of skinheads on the other. The caption reads, 'Got a problem, chaps?'

It's only ten o'clock, and Two Livers is hitting the Evian already. She has one of her biggest days ahead of her since joining Grossbank, and she's spooked because last night someone called in the early hours and told her they know where she lives.

'That was Dan Harriman. He's a wanker!'

She looks at me with pity. I don't like it when she looks at me that way. 'It wasn't Dan Harriman. I was with Dan Harriman.'

'You… were with… Dan Harriman?'

'Why not? Who were you with?'

'That's different. I'm the boss.'

'Oh sure, boss, I forgot.'

And then I start to think.

'Maria!'

'Yes, Mister Hart?'

'How long would it take someone to find my home address?'

'Five minutes, perhaps less. If they had access to the internet. Do you want me to show you?'

'No. What about my phone number?'

'Are you in the book?'

I've no idea if I'm 'in the book' – Wendy always dealt with that sort of thing.

'Possibly.'

'Then about thirty seconds.'

'What if I'm not?'

'Harder. They'd have to get inventive. Probably not impossible though. Do you want me to find out?'

'No. But I tell you what – call my lawyers, tell them Wendy can have the flat after all, but I need signed papers by this afternoon, because this is definitely it. My final, final offer. Then call my real estate agent and tell him to raise the bid on the house in Holland Park, but I'm going to want to buy it through an overseas holding company.'

Now I'm spooked too. It's great to play these games, but nothing's actually supposed to happen. Not to people like us, anyway.

A succession of visitors are arriving downstairs, and Two Livers goes down to greet them. Six out of the UK's seven largest pharmaceutical and healthcare companies are meeting today at Grossbank's offices. The exception is Eastern Pharma. Their management are on a roadshow in the States, but their Chairman is getting up early to join us by video-conference.

When Two Livers shows them into the large conference room, I'm stuck on the phone in the corner and shrug apologetically.

'Yes, Secretary of State, yes.' I look at them as they take their places. 'They're here now. We just need to get Eastern Pharma on the video-link, then we'll kick off. I'll pass that on. Thank you, Secretary of State.'

I hang up. 'Gentlemen I'm sorry – politicians do rather like the sound of their own voices.'

I can see they're curious, but don't elaborate. I told Maria before the call that she shouldn't get used to being addressed that way, because I didn't intend to make a habit of it. Two Livers does the intros and organises coffee for everyone else and a large bottle of Perrier – brought in by her rather nervous assistant – for herself. Finally we call up California and get a bleary-eyed, elderly suit on the video-link, who is apparently Sir Crispin Monk, Chairman of Eastern Pharma.

'Gentlemen, thank you for coming here today, and a special thank you to you, Sir Crispin, for joining us so early in your morning. We're here to discuss follow-up to yesterday's announcement concerning Hastings BioScience, which I know everyone on this side of the Atlantic has read about in today's newspapers.'

'And over here too.' The face on the screen is slightly out of sync with the voice, but Sir Crispin is holding up a copy of the *Wall Street News*, pointing to a small piece on the front page. 'Grossbank has been very courageous. I didn't think the Germans had it in them, but I suppose it's down to you. Our chaps have been pretty hopeless on this, and the Yanks haven't been seen for dust.'

Music to my ears. Two Livers is smiling smugly.

'Thank you, Sir Crispin. Your kind words are greatly appreciated. But words sadly are not enough. Grossbank has put its neck on the line to maintain a world class testing facility here in the UK that is vital to all of your businesses, both now and in the future. We're taking a risk not just corporately, but personally as well – because we believe in this. But we can't do it alone. If everyone else says, "Great, Grossbank have got us off the hook, we're in the clear", and the AFF come after us and our staff the way they went after HBS, it will only be a matter of time before Frankfurt loses its nerve. We need to send Frankfurt a signal – a clear and unequivocal signal – that we're not alone here, that others appreciate what we're doing and will support us.'

One of the men sitting around the table interrupts at this point. 'So what are you looking for from us? A public statement?'

'No. Like I said, words are cheap.' I point to the telephone. 'I have it on good authority that the British government is going to be behind us all the way on this. Government support doesn't necessarily count for much in some sectors, but healthcare is different. We have a lot of goodwill there, and when it comes to things like accelerating approvals for new drugs, or getting the National Health Service to adopt a new product, we'll be well placed to help the companies we're working with.'

The suits around the table sit back, pondering what I'm saying, and wondering if that really was Joanna Harriet, the Secretary of State for Health, on the phone.

'The trouble is, we're not working with any at the moment.'

'So you want our business?'

'Investment banks always want your business, and we're no different. But what we want – what we need – is your endorsement of Grossbank, and what we're doing. And the best endorsement, the one that speaks volumes to the world, is when you appoint us to lead, or participate in, major transactions on your behalf. If HBS means anything at all to you, at least give us a shot.'

'You're right.' It's Sir Crispin, his lips still out of sync with his voice. I wonder if it's the video-link, or something he's on. Maybe I could get like that, if I keep playing every night. 'Eastern Pharma is floating its US subsidiary on the New York Stock Exchange. We're over here roadshowing the company to investors right now. Hardman Stoney are leading the deal for us. I'm going to tell them I'm appointing Grossbank alongside them. I don't care if you perform in the deal or not. It's about making a statement.'

Bingo! Two Livers is smiling to herself. Was it really me who swung him? She avoids my eye. And takes another sip of Perrier.

I'm about to thank Sir Crispin, when I realise he's saying something else. 'Eric? Is that you sitting there?'

One of the suits nods and says yes.

'Well, you should put Grossbank into the project financing for your new Turkish manufacturing plant. You're using Bartons, aren't you? Where were they when the chips were down?'

And so it goes on. Sir Crispin is unstoppable. He goes around the table, pinning them down one after the other. A lease financing here, a bond issue there, some of them significant, others more symbolic. By the end, when I'm showing them out, and assuring them that I'll give the Secretary of State a full briefing, we've created the basis for launching Grossbank as a major force in global health-care investment banking.

Christ, I'm good.

When the last of them has gone, I nudge Two Livers and grin. 'I don't know what Sir Crispin was on, but he was flying today – what a star. We should form a global healthcare advisory board, make him chair of it, and hold meetings twice a year in the Bahamas and Zermatt. Just as a reward for today.'

She waves her hand dismissively. 'No need.'

'No need? Why not?'

She winks at me. 'Sir Crispin and I go back a long way.'

Damn, this girl's an operator.

I report in to Herman to give him ammunition in the continuing war against Biedermann, which has taken a turn for the worse with several bank employees hurt in a demonstration outside the Grossbank Tower by eco protesters, anti-capitalists and other radical groups.

'Look at it this way, Herman – at least everyone's heard of us now.'

He doesn't see the funny side.

I return to my desk for an interview with a cute female reporter for *Her* magazine. She asks me a bunch of dumb questions about what it's like to be a hero, and can I sleep at night, worrying about what AFF extremists might do to me. Honey, I never sleep at night. Why waste time? I've got far better things to do. She asks me if finance is boring.

'Finance is the sex of the twenty-first century.'

'Really? Can I quote you on that?'

Sure, if you want to, but everyone will know it's not true. Sex is the sex of the twenty-first century, and if you don't believe me, ask Ilyana, and Nina, and Carla, and Breathless Beth…

♦ ♦ ♦

Tonight is different. Tonight I'm not going to shag hookers, or if I do, it won't be until much later. Tonight I have a date. I'm meeting Sally Mills, and I intend to give her every opportunity to show me just how grateful she is for saving her brother's bacon.

When I leave the office at around six-thirty there are a small group of animal rights protesters standing behind a barrier with several policemen and some of Grossbank's private security guards preventing them from interfering with employees. I'm tempted to follow the example of some of our traders and wave a fistful of fifty pound notes at them, but apparently it's considered provocative. I collect H1 PAY from the underground car-park next to the building – similarly protected by police and private security guards – and head south and then west along the Embankment. I'm meeting Sally at the Savoy, on the grounds that some of my most successful seductions have started with drinks in the American Bar.

She's as beautiful as ever, in fact even more so. I realise I've never really seen her like this, when she's made a special effort. She's wearing a simple black mid-length dress, strapless, with a pearl necklace and earrings, and she's put her hair up. The effect is simple, designer-free and elegant. I don't ask where Trevor is.

She starts by thanking me again for all I've done for Harry. He's apparently like a new man. His whole team have been re-energised. No-one believed that a firm like Grossbank would come to the rescue.

Neither did I, but I don't say that.

We have a couple of cocktails in the bar, then wander through to the restaurant for dinner. Conversation is remarkably easy, but I feel like there's an elephant in the drawing room, and we're both pretending it's not there.

By the end of dinner I'm feeling completely relaxed – always a dangerous state – she's slightly flushed from what for her is probably an unusual amount of alcohol, and as we sip our coffee it seems to me the time has come to find out where I stand. Will I rip her panties off or not?

'Sally – it's been wonderful tonight. All that I hoped for.' Except a blow-job. At least so far. 'But there's something I need to ask you. You know my feelings for you. I've got you in my head and I can't let go. I want you. I don't want to scare you, and I don't want you not to see me again, but all I can do is be honest with you. It's the truth, Sally – I'm in love with you.'

She puts her napkin to her eyes and starts sobbing. 'Oh, Dave, don't. Please don't.' She looks at me helplessly. 'I can't. It would be wrong. For me, for you, for Trevor, for the boys. It's not that I don't have strong feelings for you – what woman wouldn't?' Quite. 'But I can't. I'm sorry.'

Before I can start the line about it sometimes being right to go with your feelings, to trust your instincts, even if only for a single night, the maitre d' appears and asks if the young lady is all right. Then someone at another table points at me and says, 'Isn't that Dave Hart, the banker who's taking on the Animal Freedom Front?' and all heads are turning our way, some discreetly, some not caring, and a couple of schmucks from another table come over to shake my hand and ask if they can buy us a drink. Damnation. The moment is gone. Furious, I decide to call it a day.

The doorman drives H1 PAY round to the front of the hotel, holds the door for Sally, while I let myself in, and I slip him a fiver for his trouble. It's gone midnight, it's been raining, and we drive in silence through the dark, almost empty streets. Sally's staying with her cousin, who lives in Bermondsey, so I head south to drop her off, inwardly seething that this means still more delay before I can call Nina and Beth and get the evening properly underway.

There aren't many cars around as we head into a part of London that I'm not familiar with. The Bentley has a satnav that keeps me on the right route, but a couple of times when I'm stopped at traffic lights I imagine I see a car some way behind me slowing down, keeping its distance.

Snap out of it, Hart – you'll be seeing greens under the bed next. We drive on, until we reach another set of lights.

That's when everything goes pear-shaped. As I'm slowing for the lights, an anonymous, battered white van comes up fast behind us. I see its lights in the mirror, and assume it's going to slow down. But it doesn't, and I brace myself as it smashes into the back of the Bentley, pushing us forward across the road and into a wall. The front hits the wall and crumples, while the air bags explode in front of us.

I'm not sure exactly what happens next, but I remember looking at Sally, who's lying against the passenger door, her eyes shut, as my door opens, someone reaches over to undo my seatbelt, and I'm yanked out of the car. Part of me thinks I'm being helped, but as I stand unsteadily beside the car a fist smashes into my stomach, winding me so that I crumple slowly to the floor.

I'm lying on the wet road, my cheek resting on the ground, looking at a pair of Doc Martens. A voice says, 'Look at the City's not-so-hard man now.' I look up and count six of them, standing around me. Five men and what is theoretically a woman, though she barely qualifies. Combat jackets and jeans, shaven heads or long, dyed hair, boots and gloves. One of them has a baseball bat, and another has a long length of chain. The one standing nearest to me pulls out a flick knife and clicks it open. He grins, a dirty-toothed, bad breath grin. 'Say night-night, big Dave – it's lights out time.' I groan and try to push myself to my feet. I hear another voice.

'We goin' to do her, too?'

'Yeah.'

'NO!' I surprise myself as I leap to my feet, nearly overbalance, and swing my right fist – straight into the wall. A fierce pain shoots through my arm as I stagger back, stung as much by the scornful laughter that greets my attempt at heroics. I run at the nearest one, grab his jacket, and find myself spinning round as he twists and throws me to the ground. I lash out and my left fist smashes into the road surface. One of them kicks me in the stomach, and I groan and choke back tears.

They are hysterical with laughter now as I desperately fish for my mobile phone in my jacket pocket and start dialling.

The leader squats beside me and watches me dial. 'Go ahead, big Dave – call the police. Average response time, this part of town? I'd say about ten minutes. They don't really want to get here any sooner, see?'

I can hear a voice at the other end, and I start repeating over and over the name on the street sign on the corner. I'm still half dazed, still in shock.

That's why I'm not too clear what happened next.

A powerful engine, tyres screeching, doors opening, and I roll over to see a dark coloured car, a Range Rover, stopped in the middle of the road. Four men get out, average height, slim build, short hair, probably late twenties to mid-thirties, wearing anonymous dark suits and ties. They're not rushing, but they don't hesitate.

One of them approaches the thug with the baseball bat, who raises it and steps forward to take a swing at him. The man in the suit parries and sweeps the bat away, then brings his other hand into the thug's ribs. He does a one, two, three burst of rib-cracking punches, a swift karate chop to the neck, so that the thug goes down, all without breaking step, speaking or catching his breath. Then he's on to the woman, who yells at him and swings her fist, but he parries again, gives her a stiff-finger jab to the throat which leaves her clutching her neck, gasping and making horrible suffocating sounds, then doubles her up with a punch to the stomach, and as she falls to her knees steps around her and gives a one, two, three to the kidneys. She collapses to the ground, heaving for breath and making horrible, unnatural sounds. Four against six takes about fifteen seconds, though time isn't working for me the way it usually does. There are no dramatic kung fu kicks or thuggish head-butts, as far as I can see no blood, not even any words exchanged. One of the eco's screams something at them, but he's cut off mid-shout by a karate chop. And then there are only crumpled bodies on the ground.

One of the men from the Range Rover kneels beside me. 'Mister Hart, are you all right?'

I nod yes, and he helps me to my feet. 'Check her. In the car...'

One of them opens the passenger door, leans in and then calls across. 'Fine. Bump on the head.'

They turn as we hear a police siren faintly in the distance. The one who's holding me pats me on the shoulder. 'Mister Hart, Mike Moss sent us. He said you might need looking after. You'll be fine now. But we need to go. We don't work in the UK, only overseas.'

They walk – do these people ever run? – to the Range Rover, climb in and start the engine. One window slides down. 'You'll be fine – just don't mention us.'

The Range Rover roars off around the corner as I stand, unsteady on my feet, and look at the crumpled bodies all around me. I stagger over to check on Sally, who is unconscious, but still breathing. The minutes tick slowly past while the distant sirens get closer. One of the eco's starts moaning on the ground a few yards away, lifts his head and starts coughing up blood. With all the strength I can muster, fuelled by fear and pain and humiliation, I kick him in the head, just as a police car pulls up beside me, its flashing blue light casting a surreal effect all around. The doors open, and two policemen step out, one of them talking on a handheld radio.

'Roger, control, a silver grey Bentley Azure, registration Hotel One Papa Alpha Yankee. I recognise the driver from the papers. It's that Dave Hart, the bloke who's taking on the AFF. Looks like he took 'em on tonight, all right. You're not going to believe this...'

◆ ◆ ◆

Another day, another dollar. Or in my case, another great heroic deed. If Sally Mills doesn't have sex with me after this, I may join a monastery.

I'm not pressing charges against the AFF, although the police are still considering their own position on charging them, and the AFF members are sticking to their code of omerta.

Which may be just as well, because it would ruin a great story.

With the police and the ambulances last night came the usual press pack, tipped off by chums on the inside. The *Post* has a front page picture of me standing by an ambulance, having my knuckles bandaged by a paramedic, next to a line of unconscious bodies on stretchers: *Chopper Hart Nails AFF*. I'm 'Chopper' now – another label! I hope people understand it's because of the incident in Jamaica, and nothing to do with whatever might happen late at night between consenting adults. It was too late for all but the last editions, but I'm the lead story on the radio and TV news.

That's the good part. The bad part is Trevor the teacher. Sally has mild concussion and so I get to call him from the hospital, dialling 'Home' from the mobile phone in her handbag. He thought she was at her cousin's. I explain that she wanted to tell me more about Harry and HBS, that we overran so decided to eat and then I was driving her back to her cousin's when it all happened. It's hard to tell if he believes me. When he arrives he stares around the ward, never having seen one before.

I'm too exhilarated to sleep, having just had a terrifying near death experience, so after calling the AA to remove my badly injured H1 PAY, around three a.m. I take a cab to the flat that Nina and Beth share in South Ken and have a party.

By the time I get into the office, around ten-thirty, everyone wants to speak to me. Even the ones who don't want to speak to me want to glance surreptitiously at my bandaged knuckles.

I call Mike Moss and thank him, and say how awkward it is having everyone think that was my work last night. He chuckles and says it's a double whammy – it got me off the hook, and people might think twice about having a go at me in future.

The Silver Fox has gone into overdrive. He has a whole series of interviews lined up for profile pieces, the TV people want me on the *Dick and Sally* show, and will I appear on *Finance Today*?

Everyone is calling. Even Herman congratulates me. 'Dave, you are astonishing. How did you do this? Are you all right? I thought this sort of super-hero action only happened in the movies.' It does. The conversation drags on. I know last night was impressive, but I can sense there's something more on his mind.

In the end he can't resist telling me. 'Have you heard about Doktor Biedermann? He heard what happened to you, and he's gone into hiding. Just for the moment. It's on the advice of the bank's security department.' There's one particularly juicy item that he just has to pass on. 'Oh, and he has changed his office too, with all of his photographs and mementos, since his visit to London. In fact a number of board members have. Word seems to have spread fast in Frankfurt about your ironic pastiche. So self-deprecating. So typically British. Such humour.'

Ironic? Self-deprecating? Me? I glance at my 'Me Wall'. Damn, I'll have to change it now. Maybe I'll ask Samantha to give me back the photo of me with Madonna.

Wendy calls, but I tell Maria to take a message. Tripod Turner sends a huge novelty condom filled with helium to float around my office – 'For the biggest swinging dick in town'. Dan Harriman is apparently indisposed, but sends two hookers to the office dressed as policewomen, but security don't let them through, and I send flowers to Sally in hospital, with a message saying I will never, ever let anyone hurt her. Realising she's concussed and may not remember what actually happened, I enclose a short letter in a sealed envelope as well, ambiguously stating how what happened last night will be forever etched in my memory. It's true, after all. And if she misunderstands and thinks we might have already had sex, it might not be such a struggle second time around.

After a night like last night, some people might take a day off. But in the fast moving world of investment banking, you go forward or die. And anyway, I'd only spend it with my chiropractor or my acupuncturist, and I'm tired enough already. After another meeting with the police, signing more statements, and a couple of press interviews, it's back to business.

I have a meeting scheduled, with Two Livers, at three o'clock at the Meridien Hotel on Piccadilly. Biedermann has told people in Frankfurt that we still haven't won any 'real' corporate clients. He told Herman that MOSS was a one-off, and doesn't count because no other firm would take it on. HBS doesn't count either, because it was a basket case, and no other firm had management suicidal enough to want it. So now Two Livers and I are going to win a piece of real business.

The Old Orinoco Trading and Investment Company is straight out of a time warp. It's a Columbian company, state-owned, and for years was run as a private fiefdom for successive Presidents and their friends and families. But now, in a sign of the times, they are looking at a partial privatisation by way of listing their shares on an overseas stock exchange. Their senior management are in London for a beauty parade of investment banks. They own vast amounts of agricultural land, timber and mineral rights. With the right strategy, this company could be worth billions. Every major investment bank in town is after them, and quite why they'd ever give us the business is beyond me.

But that won't stop us trying.

We arrive to find the meeting schedule is already running late, and a team from Schleppenheim are in the anteroom waiting to go on. They are sitting around drinking coffee and chatting, looking buttoned-up and preppy. The conversation stops as soon as I show up.

'Aren't you Dave Hart?' The team leader, an early forties MD, puts down the paper he was reading about my adventures last night. I nod. My hands are starting to ache, my stomach is hurting from where I was punched and kicked, and I'm feeling very tired and short-tempered.

He obviously wants to make conversation, probably so he can tell his buddies that he was chatting to Dave Hart today. Isn't that something? Six months ago, he'd probably never heard of Dave Hart, or if he had, thought Dave Hart was some anonymous, middle-ranking turkey in Rory's team at Bartons.

I sit on one of the couches with Two Livers, and slowly – and rather painfully – start unwrapping the bandages around my left hand. This fascinates everyone in the room, and they even start wincing in sympathy as I have to tug to pull them free from the scabs that have formed on my knuckles.

The team leader approaches again. 'Painful?'

I wince as the scab on my forefinger splits open and starts bleeding. 'No.'

He turns to Two Livers, perhaps wondering if she might be easier conversation. 'So it's just the two of you?'

She glances across at his team of five. 'That's about equal.'

He grins and nods, and I want to give her a high five, but I'm too absorbed in what I'm doing.

Two Livers ignores him and turns to me.

'So Dan wanted anal sex again last night.'

'Really?' I barely raise an eyebrow. The schmuck from Schleppenheim is standing by us, clearly taken aback by the turn in the conversation, not sure if he should join in or move away. His team are looking at him standing there like a dork, wondering what he'll do.

'I've lost count of the number of times I told him I think it's disgusting. He comes up with all these lines about how everyone does it, you use lots of gel, it might be painful at first, but you get used to it.' She looks round suddenly, and the team from Schleppenheim instantly do very poor impressions of reading newspapers, glancing through their pitch books and staring out of the window. The schmuck self-consciously ambles back and sits down on a couch.

'So I got Claude round.'

'Claude?'

'My friend from Haiti. Male model. Six-foot ten, black guy. Swinger.'

'What for?'

'I told Dan okay, we'd do it, but first I wanted to play some new games. I handcuffed him to the bed. Face down. Wrists and ankles.'

You can hear a pin drop. When one of the Schleppenheim team turns over a page in his newspaper, the rest glare at him.

'Handcuffs? Really?' I'm still picking at my scabs. 'Face down? What did he think was going to happen?'

'Massage.'

'So did you oil him up?'

'Sure. Then I let Claude in. Claude's huge. Dan got a shock. Went mad. Started screaming.'

'Really? I'm not surprised.'

'I told Dan not to worry, Claude would use lots of gel, everyone does it, it might be painful at first, but he'd get used to it.'

'Did he?'

'Not the first couple of times.'

'Will you see him again?'

'Don't think so.'

The door to the meeting room opens and a pretty receptionist type comes out. We all stand and the Schleppenheim team start to get their pitch books together.

'Excuse me.' I wander over to the receptionist, dumping my soiled bandages in a bin. 'Dave Hart, Grossbank. You may have heard, I had a rather eventful night last night. I'm not feeling my best. Would you mind if we went in next?'

The schmuck is about to protest, when Two Livers gives him a beaming smile. 'Hey come on, loosen up. You wouldn't say no to a lady, would you?'

No. He wouldn't say no to her. Nor to me. His whole team stare at us, then he shakes his head and we go through into the conference room.

Shock and awe. Moral superiority over the enemy. That's what we just achieved. Have you read *The Prince*, or *The Art of War*? Neither have I, but at least I own them.

We go through a reception room, where the girl sits, then into a large conference room with a broad oval table. We meet Oscar Rodriguez, the chairman, a short, fat, shiny-headed bald man with a big grin and the sort of suit worn by drug dealers in *Miami Vice*. He has with him his weasel-featured finance director and a couple of 'advisers', one of whom sits on his board, from the Orinoco Banking and Finance Corporation. They will work jointly on the deal with whichever bank is appointed, and Oscar has complete faith in them, partly because he also sits on their board.

Oscar has on the table in front of him several newspapers, showing photographs of last night. He begins by congratulating me, saying how I must be part-Columbian, because that is how they would deal with these people – I manage not to say that I thought they just shot them – and once again everyone is fascinated by my knuckles.

After the introductions I explain that Two Livers will give them an outline of the main issues we see facing them as they think about listing their shares, and will run through our capabilities and what we see ourselves bringing to the party. She starts talking and they stare at her breasts, her neck, her ear-lobes, her lips, her eyes, and her surprisingly strong fingers – she can do one of the best handshakes of any woman I've ever known, and I have known one or two. They take no notes, and she sits and purrs at them, unaided by any slides or handouts that might distract them.

After fifteen minutes, she's done and I ask for any questions. While they're thinking, I ask if they mind if I smoke. Oscar actually seems relieved to have met the first non-PC banker in London.

I take out a large Cohiba and put it on the table in front of Two Livers. Without blinking, she picks it up, sniffs it, rolls it between her fingers, nods that it's okay and fishes out a cigar cutter from her handbag. She places the end of the cigar in the mouth of the cutter, and looks up to catch Oscar's eye as she snaps the end off. He winces and sits up in his seat. Then she puts it in her mouth, moistening it with her lips, rolling it gently around so that the whole of the end is wet, and lights it with a lighter from her handbag. After a few puffs, she looks again at Oscar and blows a perfect smoke ring across the table at him. Then she hands me the cigar, all the while without making eye contact with me or saying a word.

'Thank you.'

'Yes,' Oscar sighs. 'Thank you.'

He motions me to get up and step over to the coffee pot on the sideboard at the end of the room. His finance director starts asking inane finance director questions of Two Livers, like how did we come to our valuation, what fees would we charge, what financial statements we'd require for the prospectus, and other such bullshit.

Oscar puts his arm around my shoulder and leans in confidentially so that we can talk.

'Are the two of you...?'

I gesture innocently towards Two Livers. 'Married? No. But we're... close.'

'Oh?'

'Yes. I'm close to all of my female employees.' I smile knowingly and wink, with a man-to-man look on my face.

He laughs and slaps me on the shoulder. 'Hombre. You are truly a man. I thought this sort of conduct was not permitted between colleagues in this country?'

'Grossbank is different. I set the rules. Any woman employee wanting to make managing director has to sleep with me at least three times. Just so I know she's good enough.'

He looks at me as if he thinks I might be joking. I stare back, dead pan.

'Hombre.' Another slap on the arm.

We take our places again, and I put another cigar on the table. 'Miss MacKay, I think Mister Rodriguez would like a cigar.'

When he shows us out, ten minutes or so later, amid much back-slapping and laughter, the Schleppenheim team get up from their seats and prepare to go in. As she passes the most junior member of their team, a nervous looking kid in his early twenties, Two Livers opens her handbag and passes him a small tin of Vaseline.

'Here – when you get inside, pass this to your boss. Tell him it might help.'

◆ ◆ ◆

Weeks have passed. Busy, hectic weeks.

Our new people are arriving in droves now, scooped from the most successful firms on the street, and paid the sort of money that creates a feeling of obligation to deliver in even the most hard-nosed cynic. Everyone has heard of us – at least, they've heard of me – and we're starting to do business, and not just in the pharma sector. It all feels remarkably like it might actually work, and when it does, people won't resent it too much, because we showed we had balls, and we did something they didn't dare to do.

As far as regular business goes, my most spectacular coup so far was a block trade. The French government decided it was going to sell its last remaining twenty per cent shareholding in Société Financière du Sud, an industrial conglomerate and holding company previously under state control.

Rather than trying to place their shares in an orderly manner, hiring a group of banks to market them carefully to institutional investors around the world, they decided to follow the latest market fad and conduct a sudden death blind auction, whereby all the large investment banks are told the deal's coming and they should prepare a bid – in strictest confidence – so that after the market closes they can compete to commit commercial suicide by buying the entire shareholding and then selling it on the next day.

The only investment bank likely to make money out of a trade like this is the one advising the government, because they're running the auction and so can't be a bidder. The others ought to laugh and give a short answer ending in 'off', but instead they work themselves up into a lather of excitement, desperate to see if they can 'win' this 'prestigious' piece of business.

The banks have discreet conversations with large institutional investors, especially hedge funds, giving them inside information about the forthcoming sale on a strictly confidential, 'no dealings' basis, to establish what investor appetite there is for the shares.

These investors, who have to be among the few people in the world even more unscrupulous than investment bankers, knowing there is a large block of shares about to hit the market, instantly start selling, knowing the price is about to fall. Hold on, you say, they just said they wouldn't deal. As if. If they don't already own the shares, they borrow them, selling something that they don't actually own but expect to be able to buy back more cheaply very soon – 'closing their short position' in the jargon of the market. Sell it for a hundred and buy it back for ninety, and you've made a ten euro turn.

When eventually the bids go in, and one lucky bank 'wins' the auction, everyone knows that the crazy idiot is going to have to scramble to unload the position, and the lucky losers also join the hedge funds in selling the stock, putting further pressure on the price, to rubbish the competition and make a little money along the way. It's a horrible situation to be in. The investment bank that wins generally loses a ton of money, the company in question sees its shares get a hammering, and only the government is happy, because it got its money. And the block trade business? As someone once said, it's a great way for investment bankers to show who has the biggest dick and the smallest brain on the block – at least until now.

What's different this time, is that Grossbank is on the list of bidders. Paul Ryan has called in a favour from an old buddy at Financial Solutions, the small advisory firm running the auction. The idea is that if people think we're bidding on a trade like this, they'll start to take us seriously. No-one expects us to win, including my own team.

Unlike the other firms bidding for the block, we aren't really in a position to talk to many hedge funds, because we hardly know any. Unlike the other firms, we don't yet have a proper sales force of brokers. Tripod Turner tells me not to touch it with a barge pole. I call Herman the German and he asks if I'm sure I know what I'm doing, and I say of course not, I hardly ever know what I'm doing, which makes him laugh. The shares close at sixty-two euros ninety, and I suggest we put in a really aggressive bid at sixty-three euros a share.

'The government holding's been overhanging the share price for months. As soon as it's gone, the price will rise. Come on - let's win this sucker. We're Grossbank - Grossbank rocks!'

It's only then that I recall that at Bartons, no-one ever took any notice of my views on bidding for blocks, or much else for that matter, so it really didn't matter what I thought. The problem is, now I'm in charge, and despite the obvious misgivings of the team, the bid goes in, to the amazement of Paul's old buddy at Financial Solutions. Since anyone with a brain is bidding at least a small discount to the closing price, we win.

Paul Ryan looks sick. 'What do we do now? We own twenty per cent of the company. First thing tomorrow everyone's going to be shorting the hell out of it, the price will go into free-fall, and if we manage to get rid of half of it, even at a huge loss, we'll be lucky. What's the plan, boss?'

I like it when he calls me boss. It's late, and I have a rendezvous with Fluffy and Thumper from the Pussy-Cat Club – beautiful Thai twins, who do an extraordinary double act guaranteed to whet even the most jaded appetite – so instead of saying how the hell should I know, I've never bid on a block trade before and I didn't expect to win, I look confident, wink and tell him we'll think about it in the morning.

He thinks I've got nerves of steel, and carries on looking sick. The reality is that I still haven't fully fathomed out exactly what I've got us into.

In the morning, the shares do indeed go into free-fall. I'm scared shitless, a rabbit caught in the headlights, everyone looks to me for a lead, and on my instructions, we do… nothing.

'Sit tight – don't lose your nerve.' No trader ever sits tight. But I'm desperately tired, it's a 3G day. I feel like I've got alcohol oozing from every pore, my whole system saturated from a night of truly excessive excess with Fluffy and Thumper, and there's a brass band marching up and down in my head. When the stock hits fifty euros a share, I panic and tell our traders to go into the market and buy a shed load more. If we own some at sixty-three euros a share, and some at fifty, our average price will be a lot lower than it was. At least that's why I keep telling myself it's a good move.

By noon, we're up to thirty per cent of the company. Herman wants to know what's going on. So does Paul. So do I.

'Let's just say it's a reverse block trade. We're not selling these shares, we're buying them.' It's a vague attempt at humour by a condemned man, as I face the imminent prospect of the whole pack of cards collapsing around me.

I say it to Paul in the middle of the trading floor, and word spreads like wild-fire. Since no investment banker can ever keep a secret, and everyone on the trading floor has at least one telephone, the word soon gets around the market.

'Grossbank isn't selling Société Financière du Sud – it's buying it!'

A couple of minutes later, reports are going across the wire that there is speculation in the market that Grossbank may be buying SFS, either acting on behalf of a potential acquirer – various names are mentioned – or possibly for its own account, as part of a foray into merchant banking-type principal investment. Herman calls.

'Are we buying SFS?'

'I don't know. Are we?'

The price is no longer in free-fall, but rising rapidly as the market gets wind of the fact that not only has the government overhang been removed, but there's a predator on the loose, hoovering up shares with a view to launching a bid. An official announcement is expected imminently. Now all the short sellers are rushing to buy shares, closing out their short positions. Sell something at sixty euros a share, and buy it back at seventy, and the trade doesn't look quite so clever, does it sucker? The institutions which actually owned SFS shares and sold them on news of the block trade are out there buying them back, not wishing to miss out on the action now that something's happening. On the trading floor at Grossbank, the traders cheer every time the price goes up another euro. At sixty-five euros, we start unloading shares, and carry on selling them as the price reaches seventy, finally losing the last of our position at seventy-three. When the French Trésor call up to ask what the hell's going on, I don't even need to lie. We've sold the whole position, and no, we have no idea where the takeover speculation came from.

Amongst our own traders, my stature and prowess have reached previously unimaginable heights. When all around were panicking, I stood there, saying nothing, doing nothing, while the stock went through the floor. Balls the size of melons, and made of steel. No wonder, because I'm Dave Hart – or Chopper as they call me now. For the first time, I hear two of my own employees saying 'Grossbank rocks' and giving each other a high five. Truly, I am a legend.

◆ ◆ ◆

I'm flying to the Fatherland again, but this time things are different. Tom, my new driver, has taken me to Northolt in the armoured, S-class Mercedes the firm is insisting I use for my own security and their well-being – I'm a key man, after all. Tom is well over six feet tall, strongly built, and if he wasn't working for Grossbank, could probably get a job with Mike Moss. I'm flying from Northolt because I'm taking a smoker – a private jet – so as to avoid the pressures and delays of public transport, and because it affords me the privacy to work on sensitive things during the flight. The sensitive thing I'll be working on during this flight is twenty-two years old and used to be an air hostess with one of the major airlines, before switching to private aviation. The bank pays a thousand pounds a trip for her to take care of me. She serves drinks and snacks during the flight, and makes sure my newspapers are on board. Anything else is a private matter between consenting adults. Honestly.

Today I'm feeling particularly pleased with myself, even by my standards. Last night I had a major coup. Wendy and I are hardly speaking since I moved out of the flat in Sloane Square and she moved in. I'm living in a large house in Holland Park, which is still in chaos while an interior designer gives it a total revamp, chooses furniture, art, books, sculptures, etc – everything a tasteful, cultured, well-rounded, successful investment banker would wish for at a certain stage in his life, but couldn't possibly find time to buy for himself.

In the meantime Wendy is getting hate mail, packages of human excrement, and even a pretend bomb from the AFF and associated nutters – all addressed to me, and all arriving at the flat. She thinks I did it on purpose. At the same time, the flat is bursting with presents I've sent round for Samantha, and Wendy is seething that my financial fortunes have improved so dramatically since joining Grossbank – and only after we signed our final settlement.

The only cloud on the horizon is Sally Mills. How any woman could be saved by a hero in single combat, taken by him to hospital, sent flowers by him, and then simply disappear off the radar screen, after he had put his neck on the line to save her brother's business, is quite beyond me. When I make enquiries, I'm astonished to learn that Trevor the teacher has quit East Hampton Comprehensive and the family have moved – not even waiting till the end of term – to Scotland.

What's going on? I have visions of flying in to a lonely Scottish farm in my Grossbank corporate helicopter, playing the *Ride of the Valkyries* over loudspeakers, and rescuing my beloved from imprisonment in the cold and clammy North.

In the meantime, and just so you know I'm not pining too hard, I'm getting through hookers at the rate of one or two a night.

So back to my coup. I haven't seen Samantha all year, but it's Easter and her new school in Belgravia has organised an Easter play, where we can all sit and coo at our little beloveds as they scamper around on stage in fancy dress and fluff their lines.

When it comes to parenting, mine is the ultimate outsourcing generation. We hire private obstetricians to make neat little cuts in our wives to take the pain out of pushing, maternity nurses to take away the sleepless nights, nannies and maids to take away the everyday drudge, kindergartens and private tutors so we don't have to read or spell or do adding up with our kids, and instructors to teach them everything from swimming and sport to dancing and drawing, all of which is terribly important, and none of which we could possibly do ourselves.

But the one thing we can't delegate is attending school functions. We fight to get our kids places at the most exclusive schools – because it shows how much we love them – and once we get them in, there's major kudos to be had from showing up at events. The bigger the swinging dick of a husband, the greater the New Age brownie points to be had from showing up to gaze adoringly as little Nathan and little Susie play two of the six snowflakes present at the birth of Christ in the school Nativity play, or in my case, Samantha plays an Easter bunny.

The problem is, school functions are an intense form of competitive sport, and without a team – in my case a wife – you can't win. It all begins way ahead of the official start time for the event, when the pushiest mothers – the fathers are always still at work – show up to claim the best seats, right at the front, so

that they can show little Nathan how much they adore him by swooning from the front row. They mark their territory with coats and bags and then disappear to form a gossipy cabal in some trendy wine bar round the corner. Naturally, they are all fully war-painted, dressed to kill, finest jewellery, hair freshly done, mani/pedi and waxing taken care of, and they scrutinise each other for the slightest flaw or weakness. The guys show up much later, stressed out with whatever they've escaped from at work, no time to shave or freshen up, still in their work clothes, and usually still on the mobile when they arrive to take the places their wives have saved for them.

Wendy and I used to be a great team, but I know she won't have kept me a seat, and it's not my style to sit at the back and look like a loser.

Fortunately, I have Tom. Tom's a fixer, a multi-talented man who can deal equally well with weirdos and nutters from the AFF or the PTA. Tom visits the school the night before the play, slips the caretaker a lazy fifty, and gives him a pile of coats, jackets, hats and gloves, all freshly acquired from the hospice shop on Sloane Avenue. When the ÜberMums appear on the night, two hours before the play is due to start, they are shocked to discover the entire front row taken.

The best is yet to come. I arrive bang on time, with the hall full, walk to the front, ignoring Wendy, who's in row three, lift a coat from one of the front seats and drop it on the floor in front of me. Then I sit down, lean back, cross my legs and relax, ignoring the tutting and muttering from behind me, the nudges and whispered comments that they hope there won't be a scene when the owner of the coat arrives.

It gets even better. Just as the play is about to start, there's a buzz of conversation from the back of the hall, and heads start turning. It's Two Livers and the turbo-babes. Two Livers has been hoovering up all the talent she can find from any of the major investment banks, to form the first female-dominated corporate finance department in the City. She arrives looking like a million dollars – courtesy of Manolo Blahnik, Prada and Versace, followed by dark-haired Nicky from

Toronto – twenty-nine years old, Harvard MBA, wearing Dolce and Gabbana with jewellery by Bulgari; fair-haired Sabine – twenty-eight years old from Italy, INSEAD MBA wearing Donna Karan with accessories by Mappin and Webb and a two-tone gold pendant from Kiki McDonough; Connie from Cologne – twenty-six years old, Chicago MBA wearing Armani with jewellery by Van Cleef and Arpels; and Marie-France from Nice – twenty-eight years old, Price Waterhouse trained accountant, wearing Dolce and Gabbana, with diamonds by Graff.

I could have brought hookers, but these girls are even better. In the City they're starting to be known as 'Hart's Angels'. If you think it's amazing what a thousand pounds can buy by way of female company, try a million. Or two.

Two Livers has told them I'm going to be hung out to dry tonight by the ex-wife, and I'm too good a man for that, so here they all are. Every woman in the hall is wondering who the hell they are, and wishing they would die, but only after they first get fat. The turbo-babes ignore the women in the hall, and the only acknowledgement any of the men get is when Nicky nods to a corporate lawyer she recognises, who then has to explain to his wife sitting beside him that they work on merger and acquisition deals together.

Two Livers and the babes greet me, paying homage with a kiss on both cheeks while I remain seated and acknowledge them with a nod, godfather-like, and then they similarly discard the clothing from their seats and join me in the front row.

The very best of all happens half way through the performance. The girls and I are clapping Samantha, ensuring that anything she does is greeted with even more flashes from digital cameras than anyone else, when the Chairwoman of the PTA starts coughing. She's seething in the second row, fuming that for the first time she doesn't have an uninterrupted view of darling Abigail, when she has a serious coughing fit. Without asking, she grabs the small bottle of Evian that Two Livers has placed discreetly under her chair, and takes a long swig. Then she really starts coughing, goes red, starts gasping, eyes watering, mascara running, pointing to her throat, unable to speak, and is helped from the hall mid-performance by her unfortunate husband.

There are drinks afterwards, at which I am surrounded by some of the most beautiful, glamorous women in London, all of whom have brains the size of planets. This is so far outside the normal social order, that most of the mothers retreat hissing to the corners, while the more adventurous husbands try to engage the babes in chit-chat, rapidly backing off when they find themselves interrogated about why they haven't made partner yet, or when their firm's stock is going to start trading in line with their competitors. Nicky takes a call from New York, and Two Livers and Sabine are discussing a proposal for a Japanese private placement, and it's all just so intimidating that Wendy leaves with Samantha without stopping by to say hello.

♦ ♦ ♦

My trip to Frankfurt coincides with Doktor Biedermann's emergence from hiding, after what can only be described as a sustained campaign of terror and intimidation by the extreme wing of the German radical movement. They flour-bombed him when he was giving a talk to university students, threw paint bombs at his house in the suburbs of Frankfurt, and tipped pig swill over him on a visit to the opera. He has born it all stoically, living with police protection in a constant state of nervousness, reminded by his security advisers that he has to be lucky all the time, the bad guys only need to get lucky once.

And what is it that kept him going when another man would have caved in to the pressure, resigned from the board and gone into hiding on a South Sea island?

Me. Dave Hart. The man he loathes above all others. The man behind Grossbank's extraordinary success – yes, success – in investment banking. As I take the elevator to the fifty-fourth floor, I wonder if the doors will open and he'll be waiting for me with a machine-gun.

Things would be going well for me if only I didn't feel so constantly tired. I've been running on empty for so long that my brain feels permanently fuzzy. I've twice fallen asleep in meetings, and worse still, I've started falling asleep in bed, when I had quite different things in mind. My eyes seem to be shrinking back into the dark circles that surround them, I have a permanent cold and runny nose – probably because I am so run down - and nothing seems capable of lifting me for long.

I feel desperately in need of a buzz, of something to raise my spirits and boost my energy levels again. Instead, I meet Doktor Biedermann in the corridor, muttering quietly to the fossils, while an uncomfortable Herman looks on, obviously the outsider.

'Dave – how are you? Welcome to Frankfurt.' At least he's pleased to see me. Biedermann just scowls.

I hand my coat to one of the All Germany Ladies Piano Throwing Team and we go into Biedermann's office. His 'Me Wall' is gone, and instead there are vivid splashes of red paint all over the wall and the back of the door.

'Doktor Biedermann, did you commission this?'

One of the fossils chokes back a laugh. Probably the most excitement he's had in decades. No wonder they like coming to my meetings.

'No. One of our junior employees did this. Someone who was… unduly influenced by things he read in the media.' Oh. But there's more. 'I suppose you've heard the news from Gruenkraut?'

Now both the fossils are trying not to laugh, but their shoulders are shaking and Biedermann has a nervous tic in his cheek. Herman is studying his fingernails.

'Gruenkraut? You mean from…' I search for the name, without success.

'Jan Hagelmann, my nephew.'

I snap my fingers. 'Exactly. Jan – a great kid. No, I haven't. How's he doing?'

'Very well. Your theory was correct. He has been very successful.'

I feel sure it's a wind-up, because there is no way that an arrogant little shit like Hagelmann could have found any new business opportunities in a village of seven hundred people.

'Have you heard of a computer game called *Spectres of the Night*?'

I start to wonder if the pressure has finally got to him.

'Should I?'

Well, you will, Mister Hart, believe me, you will.'

'May I ask why?'

'Because it was designed by a computer programmer in Gruenkraut. It's a live, real-time fantasy computer game played each night by millions of people all over the world, and managed from a farmhouse in Gruenkraut. My nephew met the founder and creator on his first night there, and now they are charging the players ten Euros each month by subscription, and my nephew is to be Chief Executive with twenty-five per cent of the company, and they will float on the stock exchange in a few months' time.'

This has to be a wind-up. 'Well, you must be very pleased.'

'No! I am not pleased. My nephew is planning to leave the bank.'

Well you would, wouldn't you? 'I see. But Jan will become very rich. And floating a high tech entertainment company like that is great business for the bank.'

'Money is not everything, Mister Hart.' He looks at me. 'Too much money too soon can be bad for you. Especially for such a young man. And the bank will not be floating the company.'

'Really? Who's he using?'

'Hardman Stoney. They have been waiting to break into the German market for years.' He turns and stares out of the window, his head bowed in shame. If only I had a revolver with one bullet in it, I'd pass it to him now.

'Is it something I did? When he was working for me?'

Biedermann sighs. 'No. He always wanted to rebel. Now he can. His mother –

my sister – is heartbroken. He has grown very pale, he does not shave or cut his hair, he only plays computer games night after night. And it is making him very rich.'

Isn't life a bitch? I don't know where the conversation can go after this, unless I offer to send round some hookers to bring him back to reality. Knowing Biedermann just a little, I decide instead to move on to the business report. But his heart isn't in it any more.

When I tell him we've been appointed to float the Old Orinoco Trading and Investment Company, beating off competition from the likes of Schleppenheim to do it, he simply nods and says 'Congratulations'. When I say that their partner bank, Orinoco Banking and Finance, have started doing huge volumes of share trading through us, he doesn't react. Even Herman looks sad. If this is victory, it sucks.

♦ ♦ ♦

More weeks pass, weeks that turn into months, more success, greater profits, not dozens but hundreds of new faces, and amazingly, in such a short time, Grossbank is turning into a winner. Our people walk into pitch meetings expecting to win the business. The competition actually take us seriously now. It's amazing what happens if you hire hundreds of talented people and turn them loose to do their thing. Or at least, if you're lucky enough to hire the people who hire hundreds of talented other people. I'm surrounded by so much talent now that I no longer have anything to do. Except be in charge, which is of course important – I keep telling myself I'm still the most important man in the firm. Early next year, the new building will be ready and we'll all move down to Canary Wharf. It's an extraordinary success story.

And inevitably, I'm bored. These days I take it for granted that people know who I am, that I have to live in a secure bubble, insulated both from specific

hatred directed towards me, and from the more mundane realities of everyday life. I have monthly meetings with Scotland Yard to review security, both at the bank and at home – not just the AFF, apparently the Yardies might still be a concern too. I no longer have problems with restaurant bookings, or the need to use public transport, or getting my expense claims signed off. I've arrived.

And I can't tell you how dull life is. The only person who might have livened it up, Sally perfectly-white-panties Mills, is in Scotland, refusing all contact with me, living with the appalling Trevor the non-achiever. I could offer her millions, and instead all she wants is a fucking schoolteacher.

Paul Ryan is sitting in my office, going through risk positions after the market close. Orinoco Banking and Finance have turned out to be a huge client of the Equities and Fixed Income businesses, taking massive positions, placing hugely aggressive bets that markets will go in one direction or another. More recently, they've introduced us to a clutch of Middle Eastern banking institutions that they work with, most of whom we'd never heard of before, and who have turned out to be almost as big. Paul calls them the Dodgy Dozen, and he worries that if they were to lose serious money they might default, but in the meantime, the profit we're making from them is huge. Right now, they are all lining up to short the market, betting that the current bull run is going to come to an abrupt halt and the market will fall. They're bucking the trend, betting against everyone else in huge size. I call Tripod Turner and ask what he thinks.

'Anyone shorting this market needs his head examined. We're in a bull cycle and there's a good ten per cent still to run, maybe more. The only thing that could stop it is a bomb going off.'

That's when the bomb goes off.

It's quite a large bomb, enough to bring down half the newly refurbished Department of Trade and Industry building in Whitehall. Luckily – or maybe not - it's after six o'clock, and the building is empty.

The effect on world markets is instantaneous. New York goes briefly into freefall, as terrorist alerts go off all around the world. The Prime Minister is taken to a secure bunker, although sadly he's released the next day, armed police are everywhere on the streets of London and other major capitals, and markets are in a tail-spin.

The Dodgy Dozen are about the only people around with smiles on their faces.

When I get together with Paul the following morning, they have booked paper profits of over a billion euros. He's not a happy man.

'This sucks. Everyone else has taken a bath. Including our own traders.'

The giant news screens on the trading floor are showing a video tape released to a Middle Eastern news agency of a guy with a beard in Arab dress sitting in a cave somewhere saying they did it, and there's more to come. What is it with these people? Why spoil things? Why can't they just be happy with drugs and booze and hookers like the rest of us?

'What do we really know about the Orinoco Banking and Finance Corporation?'

Paul shrugs. 'They're very big in Columbia, have a lot of Middle East connections, look after money for a bunch of wealthy Columbians, and trade very aggressively. They file all the right reports with the regulators.'

'Yeah, right.' They say that those who can do, and those who can't, teach. In the City, those who can do, and those who can't, regulate. 'And these other guys – the Dodgy Dozen?'

'Much the same. Middle Eastern money, whatever that means these days.'

'When did they put on these short positions?'

'Two days ago.'

'This sucks. Let's get the police in.'

Now Paul looks troubled. 'Are you sure? What if they did know this was coming? Do you really want to get on the wrong side of people like this? Weren't the Jamaicans and the AFF enough? We could just let them take their profits, carry on quietly trading with them, and if you really feel uncomfortable, write a big cheque to some charity or other.'

Even as he says this, he knows it won't work. I'm Dave Hart, womaniser, drug addict, alcoholic and super-hero. And I'm bored.

◆ ◆ ◆

The plods are as uninspiring as you might expect people to be who never make six figures, let alone getting a shot at real money. The Detective Chief Inspector is possibly the only person I've ever shown into my office who thinks the 'Me Wall' is real: 'My goodness, Mister Hart, you do get around.'

But when it comes to markets, this guy's an expert. While his sergeant sits taking notes, he explains to Paul and me that a lot of rumours went around the market after the DTI bombing, about possible terrorist activity behind the scenes, about how the big supporters of Middle Eastern terror might be cashing in and shorting the market ahead of the latest outrage, but it really is a conspiracy theory too far, and besides, they have 'intelligence' – really? – that shows we don't have to concern ourselves too much. He doesn't quite tell us not to worry our pretty little heads about all this, because the big boys are in charge, but he comes close.

Afterwards, when Maria has shown them out, Paul looks relieved. 'There, we've done our bit. No-one can ever say we didn't try. We told the police. They're the professionals, it's down to them now.' Arse well and truly covered, let's carry on trading. He gets up to leave.

'I'm not honouring those trades.'

Paul's half way out the door, but stops in his tracks and turns.

'You what?'

'Those trades. The billion plus euros of profit the Dodgy Dozen booked. I'm tearing up the tickets. They're not getting the money.'

'You can't do that. They'd sue. We'd be closed down. Our word is our bond. You can't renege on a trade after you've dealt.'

'I just did.'

'Dave, this is insane. What about the billion? Are you keeping that, too?'

'I'm going to bring in a group of wise men – the Bank of England, the regulators, PC Plod if he wants to be part of it – because I'm not satisfied about the bona fides of the Dodgy Dozen. I don't want you to do any more trades for these guys without my say-so. We'll sit on the money until the wise men give us a green light. And if they don't, we won't keep a penny. The whole lot goes to charity. I don't care if we get the biggest lawsuit in the world. We're Grossbank, and we're taking these guys on.'

Some bosses would delegate the task of breaking the happy news to the Dodgy Dozen, but I'm Dave Hart, and I love this stuff. We do a whole series of conference calls, tape recorded, to explain that we are investigating discrepancies in trading patterns around the time of the DTI bombing, that the British authorities are involved, and in the meantime they can whistle for their money.

Their reactions range from puzzlement and disbelief, to rage and fury. The President of one of them, sitting in Beirut, tells me I'm a Zionist motherfucker and I'd better watch my back. Another assures me that I have no idea what I'm getting into, and if I'm really going to do this, then I must be crazy. I lean close to the speaker-phone, and in a hushed voice, whisper to him, 'Say, Mister al-Fawaz, do you hear the voices, too?'

Herman is concerned. 'Are you sure about this, Dave? Are you sure about what you're getting us into?'

Of course not, Herman. I don't have a fucking clue, but I'm flying again. The Silver Fox organises another press conference. The room is packed, not just with the financial press, but with TV and radio and mainstream news as well.

Paul and Two Livers sit on either side of me, but they both look as if they'd rather be somewhere else.

'Ladies and gentlemen, thank you for coming today. I'm Dave Hart, global head of investment banking at Grossbank, and the man ultimately responsible for our activities in the world's markets. As you know, a number of financial institutions have voiced concerns about certain unusual trading activities in the stock market ahead of the DTI bombing. Grossbank is one of those institutions, and I am announcing today that as a result of our internal enquiries, we are freezing certain trades carried out by a number of client banks and other financial institutions based in the Middle East and Latin America. We are not naming those institutions in the interim, but are inviting the Bank of England, the City of London police and the regulatory authorities to convene a working party to examine their trading activities. Until such time as we are convinced that there is no link here to global terror, we are freezing over a billion euros in trading profits.

'Given the legal uncertainties surrounding our decision, you'll understand that there is very little I can add to what I've just told you, but I'm willing to take a few questions.'

Pandemonium. I love this job.

'Dick Harper, *Wall Street News*. Is your action legal? Isn't Grossbank effectively reneging on trades?'

'Thank you, Dick. You're right. Our legal position is… delicate. That's why we can't name the clients involved, and why we're bringing in outside help. But if it's a choice between doing the right thing, and sitting quietly on our hands, I think you know where Grossbank stands.'

'Eddie Strange, *Daily Post*. You said the clients concerned are from the Middle East and Latin America. Is there a connection? Could it be that the drug cartels are working with the terrorists? Is there an Afghan connection here?'

'It's too soon to speculate. When we can say something concrete, we will.' I look around. 'One more question?'

'Angela Hargraves, *Her* Magazine. Aren't you worried for your personal safety in taking these people on? What if the drug cartels are involved, as well as the terrorists? Aren't you being incredibly brave?'

Well, yes, actually, I am – and doesn't it set your pulse racing? 'Thank you, Angela. The man behind this decision at Grossbank is…' I flick a switch on the podium in front of me and turn to the giant screen behind. Damn. Instead of a huge picture of Herman, there's one of me, with my name in very large letters. I cast a vicious glance at the girl who runs the presentation team, but she simply shrugs helplessly and mouths 'Herman's orders.' I look at the Silver Fox, and he shrugs too. Damn, these Germans learn fast. '…it's me.' I nod modestly. 'Obviously, not just me alone, the board are right behind me on this.' A long way behind, actually. 'And so are my colleagues on the management committee in London.' I hold my hands out towards Paul and Two Livers, but they've both moved their chairs to the far ends of the stage, so they're out of camera shot.

◆ ◆ ◆

After the press conference, the chaos. The Bank of England had no idea I was going to involve them as 'wise men'. The regulators are equally baffled – no-one's ever accused them of being wise before. And PC Plod has had his head chewed off by the Commissioner for not telling him Grossbank was calling on their expertise as well. Who's going to organise this working group? How will they work? What will be their powers? Don't ask me, I just made the announcement. There are phone calls, more interviews, photo shoots. Everywhere I go, colleagues are looking nervously at me for encouragement. I grin and call out across the trading floor to our traders, 'Grossbank rocks.' They yell back and give me the thumbs up. On the giant screen TV's on the walls, there is footage of me at the press conference in our offices. We are the news. We are Grossbank.

Naturally, with a thousand and one things to do – and fortunately with lots of highly trained, competent people to do them – I tell Maria I'm taking an hour out of my day to see my acupuncturist.

Three hours later, when I get back, I'm drained. I haven't been sleeping lately, and all the excitement has caught up with me. It's turned into a 3G afternoon. I arrive back to find that I have visitors. Not from the 'wise men', as I thought, but the President of the Orinoco Banking and Finance Corporation, with a couple of his sidekicks. Paul Ryan has had them shown into a meeting room, and everyone's been waiting for me to get back.

I stifle a yawn, which some of the young guys seem to think is incredibly cool and brave. 'All right, let's see what they have to say.'

Paul has had a couple of security guards stationed outside the meeting room door.

When I go in, with Paul and Two Livers beside me, I find myself facing three villains straight from Central Casting. The President, early sixties with silver hair and a suntan, has a scar running down one side of his face that is even more impressive than mine. His two hoodlums – I mean colleagues – look like Mike Moss's cousins. One has a pock-marked face. All are wearing suits and ties and dark glasses, as if they've come straight from the set of *Reservoir Dogs*.

'Gentlemen – what an unexpected pleasure.'

The President, who is holding a pencil, snaps it in two. Silence.

We sit facing each other, three on three, and no-one says a word. If these turkeys think they can come into my office and intimidate me, in front of my own employees, they're damned right. They're scary as hell and I'm shitting myself. Where's Mike Moss when you need him? Finally the President clears his throat.

'You have something of ours, Mister Hart.'

Really? Oh, you must mean the billion. I'll just go and get it right now. Do you have a wheelbarrow, or would you like to borrow one of ours? Instead of answering, I raise a quizzical eyebrow. It's not that I don't want to say anything, just that all the excitement has so drained me physically, mentally and emotionally that I'm buckling under a wave of fatigue.

'We've come for our money, Mister Hart.'

Silence. Paul Ryan glances to his left, to see if I intend to say anything at all.

'Mister Hart! You would do well to take us seriously. Do you recall your friend Oscar Rodriguez, who first chose Grossbank to float his company? Our mutual friend, Mister Rodriguez, who was responsible for bringing us together?'

I stare at him through half-closed eyes.

'He died, Mister Hart. Someone put a bomb under his car.' He crosses himself theatrically. 'Oscar Rodriguez, his wife and driver all died.' He glances at his watch. 'In Bogota. About ten minutes ago.'

How could he possibly know that? Unless… Beside me, Two Livers gasps. She turns to me, but my eyes are closed completely now, and my head slowly sinks forward onto the table. I take a couple of breaths, followed by a loud, rasping snore.

♦ ♦ ♦

The legend has reached almost mythical proportions.

They're calling me the Ice Man now – Dave 'ice in his veins' Hart. Scotland Yard are fretting that I've made myself into too much of a target – really, just by falling asleep in a meeting? I'm always doing that these days. I was shagged out, for fuck's sake. Wendy's fretting about whether I've made a will – for Samantha, of course, not for herself. Herman the German insists that I keep a low profile for my own safety, and Mike Moss agrees with him. Even Tripod Turner says he'd think twice about having dinner with me, in case we were machine-gunned to death by drug dealers, or given a kick-start into the next world by a waiter with explosives strapped to his body. I see his point.

Everywhere I go, I travel with Tom in the armoured limo, and two carloads of heavies who stay in contact by radio. Two bodyguards stay with me in the house, and I have a panic button beside the bed. All of this is so seriously curtailing my usual activities, that I wonder whether it's time to cave – so that I can get back to drugs and hookers.

But as ever, it's the least expected line of attack that proves to be the one the enemy choose. They opt for blackmail. They want to ruin my reputation. Yes, honestly.

It's the beginning of September, the run-up to the bonus season, and it's Two Livers birthday. She's sitting at her desk, her chair pushed back, and she's reclining, eyes half closed, breathing heavily, while I'm crouching underneath the desk. Her dress is pushed up and she's not wearing any panties. You can guess the rest. I'd like to say I do this for all my employees on their birthdays, but I'd be lying.

Suddenly the door flies open, and Paul Ryan comes in. Two Livers jerks upright and smooths her dress down as he throws something on the desk.

'Have you seen these?'

'Seen what?'

'Photos of Dave – hard core photos of him with three hookers.'

There's a crunch as I bang my head on the desk, and Two Livers pushes her chair back to allow me to crawl forward on my knees and get out.

'What did you say?'

'Christ, Dave, I'm sorry – I didn't know you were there.'

'Dropped my pen. Got it now. Let me see these photos.'

Spread out on the desk are some high quality shots of me with three girls, all of us naked. There's a brunette – I think she was Katerina, from Estonia – a blonde – no idea who she was – and a black girl. I don't recall her either. We're not at my place, and I can't see enough from the shots to recognise where it was all happening, or even recall when, but boy, was it happening. There are fifteen pictures altogether, and I'm seriously impressed. Did I really do that? I could be a porn star.

'Look at this.' Paul passes me a note.

'Tell your boss to behave, or the press get these.'

Paul and Two Livers look pretty sick about the whole thing – they have these hangdog 'So what do we do now, boss' looks on their faces.

But I'm excited. So excited that I've dragged myself to the surface of my exhaustion, gasping for air, but ready to take on the world.

'Get me the Silver Fox.'

Two Livers also had a set of photos sent to her, and I had a set too. It looks as if that's it, though I can't yet be sure.

When the Silver Fox arrives, I have the gratifying and unusual task of giving him a PR assignment that even he hasn't taken on before. Meanwhile the team are worried that I'm not worried.

It takes a couple of days, but then Herman calls.

'Dave – I'm very embarrassed to have to talk to you like this, about a rather awkward and difficult, personal matter.'

I assume he has a problem. 'Herman, you can trust me. I'm a man of the world, I've seen it all – hell, I've done most of it.'

'I know you have, Dave. I have the photographs in front of me.'

Damn. So the bad guys are upping the ante. Fine with me. 'Oh, you got them? Great. What do you think?'

'What do I think? I don't know what to think.'

'But they have an impact, don't they? You can't tell me they don't challenge your perspective on investment bankers? The ugliness of global finance and the sensuality of the world that surrounds us. It's all there, Herman, and it's all for a good cause.'

'Dave, what are you talking about?'

'The calendar. The charity calendar that Ball Taittinger are preparing for us. Didn't you see my note? The children's cancer charities?'

'Dave – I'm worried about you.' Great, Herman, thanks a million. That makes two of us.

'I guess it hasn't happened yet in Germany, Herman, but in this country there's a fine tradition of the least likely people baring all for charity. The Women's Institute did it, rugby players have done it, trendy 'it' girls have done it, and now I'm doing it. It's just that I'm taking it to a new, more explicit extreme – though Ball Taittinger say they'll airbrush out the bits that go too far.' I know Herman hasn't hung up, because I can hear him breathing at the other end.

'Dave, I want to help you.'

'Then order ten thousand copies. Hang them in all the branch offices, all over Germany, and have an exhibition of the originals in the Grossbank Tower – that's what I plan to do over here. I've already called the President of the Orinoco Banking and Finance Corporation – told him he and his associates will all get personally signed copies when it's published. The City columns of the papers are going to start running the story tomorrow. Herman, this is going to be huge. And it's great for our image – it keeps us right out there, on the edge. That's where we have to be, Herman - edgy… and unpredictable… and dangerous.'

'We're dangerous enough, my friend. I can't allow you to do this.'

He hangs up. What kind of remark was that? We're Grossbank. We can do what we want, because Grossbank rocks. Doesn't it?

When I get home that night, I can't sleep. I realise I'm going through a kind of cold turkey – with all the security everywhere, I can't misbehave the way I'm used to, and my body is tormented by the absence of the poisons and the pleasures it's come to depend on. Half a bottle of whisky later I doze off on the bed, still fully clothed, but keep seeing faces hovering over me: black men with dreadlocks; ugly hate-filled faces of men and women in jeans and combat jackets carrying placards; smooth, evil men in sharp suits carrying nasty little machine-guns; and angry men with beards in Arab dress, their mad eyes filled with hatred. The rational part of my brain is wondering whether there's any other serious hate-group out there that I've somehow failed to antagonise, but I can't come up with one.

In the middle of all this, the phone rings. Thank God for that. I hope it's Dan Harriman, suggesting I sneak out and play hookey, or hooker, or something. I'm damned if I'll hide away in here forever. These schmucks think they can threaten Dave Hart? Think again, pal. You think I care? Bullshit.

'Hello, Dave, is that you?'

It's a familiar voice. Female, sweet, innocent. 'Sally! It's been so long. Where are you?'

She's crying. 'I'm here. In London. I've come back, Dave. I thought I could run far away and forget about you, but I was wrong. Wherever I went, there was news of you. You were in the papers, on the radio, on the television news at night. I couldn't escape. I've told Trevor. He's heartbroken. I don't think he'll ever understand. I feel so guilty, Dave, but I can't help myself. I love you.'

Am I dreaming or what? It can't be the drugs, and I've only had half a bottle of Scotch. This is it. I am definitely going to get inside those perfectly white cotton panties. At last. Tonight.

'Sally – where are you?'

'I'm at Euston station. I've just arrived.'

'Stay there. I'll be right over.'

I know – I should have told her to take a cab. She's only a woman, for God's sake. If it had been Ilyana, or sweaty Sveta, or Breathless Beth, or glorious Gabbie, or any of them really, I would have done. But this is Sally, and I've been waiting a long time.

I hang up, rush downstairs and grab my jacket and car keys. Tom's long since left for the evening, so I'll drive myself.

'Mister Hart, sir – where are you going?' It's one of the goons who's here for the night shift.

'Out. By myself.' I run to the front door, and step out into the street, where H1 PAY is parked.

'Mister Hart, sir – please wait a moment. Let me check the car first.' He's got a hand-held radio out and as he hurries after me, he's calling for a car to follow me.

'No time – sorry.' I definitely don't want a bunch of goons overseeing my great romantic moment.

I jump in, slam the door, put the keys in the ignition, and for a moment wonder if I should just wait a minute or two. Will it really make that great a difference? I promised Mike Moss I'd do as I was told. Fuck it. When have I ever done as I was told? Sally's waiting, and it really has been a long, hard chase.

I turn the key and there's a loud bang and a blinding white light. I feel rather than see the windscreen shatter in front of me and a great blast of hot air engulfs me.

Shit.

[Dave Hart will be back, in the final volume of the trilogy,
The Ego has Landed, in October 2007.]

First published in Great Britain by

Elliott & Thompson Ltd
27 John Street
London WC1N 2BX

Text © David Charters 2007
Photographs © Alice Rosenbaum 2007

ISBN 1 904027 56 3 (10 digit)
978 1904027 56 0 (13 digit)

First edition

Book design by Brad Thompson
Printed and bound in Spain by EG Zure